PRAISE FOR *HOSPITAL HILL*

"...an uncanny mystery/thriller that will keep readers guessing as dark secrets from an old insane asylum surface just before the hospital closes its doors forever."

~Reader Views Review

"...wonderful, descriptive cadence...a great deal of research on the subject... an outstanding job of combining bits and pieces of poignant history into an exciting tale of intrigue and suspense."

~Claire Gem, author of Phantom Traces

"...at once a historical novel based on Northampton State Hospital for the insane, a sharply drawn character study of those who could well have both worked there and been patients there, a tense mystery interwoven with what may or may not have been malevolent intentions, as well as a social commentary through her narrative of the state of mental health care in the 1950-1970 era."

~ Amazon Reader Reviews

Shadows in the Ward

Katherine Anderson

8·10·19

OTHER BOOKS BY KATHERINE ANDERSON

Hospital Hill

A Prisoner in the Asylum

Slave

SHADOWS

KATHERINE

IN THE

ANDERSON

WARD

www.thekatherineanderson.com

ISBN-13 978-1539011330
ISBN 153901133X

Cover design by Anik Sales
Cover photograph by Katherine Anderson
Author photograph by Mike Minicucci

Printed in the United States of America

*For Bruce
and for my parents.
As always, my greatest fans*

Part I

Chapter 1

"Anna Gilman?"

This was it, the moment she had been dreading for weeks; the meeting with her graduate school advisor about her internship. Everyone else in her class had already been assigned to theirs and most had gotten good spots—Worcester State Hospital, Boston Psychopathic; those with the highest GPAs landed at McLean, the only private hospital worth going for they said, but Anna didn't have a first choice, or even a second choice for that matter. She had gotten her BS at SUNY Upstate in Buffalo before moving to Massachusetts for graduate school; she knew very little about the state hospitals in Massachusetts except that they were prolific and most were stone dinosaurs that hardly inspired her to want to make a life at one.

She sat down in front of Professor Hobart and folded her hands in her lap to keep from fidgeting, glancing around the crowded office nervously.

"Miss Gilman, how are you?"

"I'm well thank you."

Hobart nodded without actually looking up at Anna. "Good. Well let's get right to it. You didn't have a preference for placement which made my life easy. We had a new addition to our list this year and I've chosen to assign you." Shuffling a few papers, Hobart pulled one out and put it in front of Anna, handing her a pen.

"Westborough? Where is that?"

"It's about a half hour southwest of here, closer to Worcester." The professor pulled out a white folder and handed that to Anna as well. "That's your packet. It gives you some general information about the internship as well as who your supervisor is, where to report. You'll be in the dorms on the hospital campus and of course you'll continue to work closely with me to make sure you're on track to graduate. Any questions?"

Anna shook her head and stared at the pile of papers in her hands, stalling as she turned it all over in her head, this new chapter of her life that she wasn't nearly prepared for.

"Now or never Miss Gilman." Professor Hobart was waiting for her sign, to make a decision. She had heard so many horror stories about failed internships, nightmare supervisors, careers ruined before they had even begun-- and yet here she was, ready to commit to a placement without any information about the hospital. As she debated, Hobart finally looked up at her and smiled encouragingly. "Don't worry Anna. You're going to be just fine."

Summoning the remains of her confidence, Anna picked up the pen and signed her name to the placement agreement, then tucked the orientation folder under her arm. She walked out of the office feeling bewildered but strangely invigorated. She had a near perfect grade point average and was graduating at the top of her class, but she had also never felt more unsure about anything in her life. In her tiny, cramped dorm room she opened up the folder and read through the cover sheet with her assignment; Valerie Martin, nursing supervisor. Looking at the date on the bottom of the letter she realized she now had less than three days to pack her things, turn in her final assignments, and get ready for the move from Lowell to Westborough.

Chapter 2

Westborough State Hospital rose up on the banks of Lake Chauncy, surrounded by farmland and corn fields. The main hospital looked as if it had been dropped in the middle of the campus as an afterthought; a yellow bird perched in the middle of a flock of cardinals. The brick was painted a not-quite-lemon hue while the older, statelier buildings were red brick. Anna's taxi brought her right to the door of Paine Hall, the female nurses' building which faced east with views of the lake and, Anna imagined, a spectacular view of the sunset. She was pleasantly surprised to find that Paine Hall was far nicer than the graduate dorms at UMASS Amherst—Anna was assigned a private room on the top floor overlooking both the lake and the walking trails that wound their way around the entire campus. The room was bright

4

and airy with a small, white wrought iron bed and the bathroom that joined her room with the one next door had a deep porcelain bathtub perfect for soaking.

Anna took her time unpacking her things, stacking her books on the floor next to the bed and tucking her pajamas under her pillow, pleased with herself that she had thought to pilfer an extra one from the UMASS dorm. When she was done settling in she walked out onto the lawn that stretched down to the banks of Lake Chauncy where the sun glinted off the water's crystalline surface. She took a deep breath in, enjoying the clean, crisp air that blanketed the campus and closed her eyes.

"The view is much better with your eyes open."

Startled, Anna's eyes flew open and she brought her hand to her throat. "Good god you scared me. Sneaking up on people isn't exactly an appropriate way to introduce yourself," she said, gaping at the young woman standing next to her who only laughed at Anna's outrage.

Holding out a hand to shake, the woman introduced herself. "Harper Westcott. And yes, my parents quite enjoyed *To Kill a Mockingbird*." She had a firm, strong grip and an easy smile that boasted of a confidence that made Anna wonder-- did she too exude that level of self-possession?

"I'm Anna Gilman. It's a pleasure to meet you." She eyed Harper carefully, thinking how strange it was that she looked so at ease in this place. "Are you an intern as well?" She knew there were only a few on campus and they were all being tossed into new employee orientation with the freshly hired ward staff.

Harper nodded. "Psychiatry. You?"

"Psychiatric nursing."

"Maybe we'll get lucky and be on the same ward." She checked her watch and looked up at the hospital. "Are you headed over to the administration building?"

"I am. Shall we?" Anna tucked her hands in the pockets of her cardigan and fell into step with Harper, the psychiatry intern with the larger than life personality. She looked at her sideways as they walked, trying to match her long, easy stride, the nearly imperceptible lift of her chin. If Anna had to guess, Harper Westcott was roughly her age and she came from money. Though she hadn't said what college she attended, Anna assumed she had an Ivy League pedigree and the family tree to match.

"So, Anna Gilman, where do you hale from?" Harper was also watching Anna as they walked, just as carefully as Anna was watching her, presumably sizing her up as well.

Anna hesitated. "I'm originally from Buffalo."

Harper threw back her head and guffawed. "Ah, the city that God hates."

"Pardon?"

"The snow. It's apocalyptic!" Harper was still laughing, her eyes sparkling as she held her hands over her midsection. "It's the only city I've ever seen that has an evacuation route for winter weather!"

"Yeah, yeah." Anna had heard every joke ever made about Buffalo and its temperamental weather. Lake effect snow was nothing to poke fun at though. Some of the storms Anna remembered from her childhood were the scariest things she had ever seen, walls of snow rushing off Lake Erie like an enemy force, burying the city in a matter of minutes, the snow so high sometimes you couldn't see out your windows.

"So what brought you to Massachusetts?" Harper asked, wiping her eyes and reigning in her laughter.

"Graduate school at UMASS Amherst. I managed a scholarship and a dorm room, both of which I needed desperately." Anna stopped herself, not wanting to say too much and encourage more questions. Regardless of how beguiling Harper Westcott was, or how entertaining-- Anna was reminded of Annie Oakley, only in a pantsuit- she wasn't keen to discuss too many details.

Harper must have sensed Anna's reluctance and did not ask any more questions. Instead she regaled Anna with tales of her own past—Wellesley (of course), Harvard med, and now a rotation at Westborough. She admitted to Anna that she hadn't been the most dedicated student but her father had been a Harvard man so with a few more than generous endowments from the Westcott family, Harper had hung on by the skin of her teeth, hence her placement at Westborough rather than a top tier like McLean.

Reaching the concrete steps they pushed through the front doors and into the foyer. Inside the hospital, at the foot of the main staircase a small group had gathered and was milling quietly about. As Anna and Harper moved into the crowd, she couldn't help noticing the sorry state of the main hall. It looked to Anna as if a number of half-baked updates had been made but not one with any thought of maintaining the building's grand architecture. The glassed in reception area was clouded over, the plexiglass nearly opaque with scratches and fingerprints, the sky blue paint already peeling, papered with notices to both visitors and staff.

A folding table with coffee, tea, and Danish had been laid out across from the main entrance and as Anna filled a paper cup with hot water and a tea bag that had seen better days, a woman in a smart pantsuit with a pressed white dress shirt climbed the stairs and turned to face everyone, clapping her hands to get the crowd's attention.

"Good morning everyone and welcome to Westborough State Hospital." A murmur of voices rippled through the crowd then quieted. "I'm Valerie Martin, clinical nursing supervisor. Dr. Brown, our head of psychiatry, is floating around here somewhere and most of you will get a chance to meet him a bit later. Now, we have a mixed group this morning as some of you are new employees and some of you are graduate interns. Pay close attention as new employees will be gathering in the conference room shortly, while all interns will be meeting with their assigned supervisors. Please remain here in the foyer and help yourself to coffee."

Anna watched as Valerie stepped back into the crowd and moved through it with an air of cool indifference.

Harper leaned in and whispered in Anna's ear, "Is that battleax the one you'll be with?"

Nodding, Anna widened her eyes and mimed slitting her throat. "I changed my mind. I think I want to be a ballerina."

"Too late now. Something wicked this way comes!" Harper turned and disappeared, leaving Anna face to face with the fierce-looking blond.

"You must be Anna Gilman." Valerie held out her hand and gripped Anna's firmly. "I'm Valerie Martin."

"Pleased to meet you Miss Martin."

"Call me Valerie. Why don't I give you a bit of a tour and then tomorrow we can meet officially and talk about what's expected of you while you're here with us."

Valerie guided Anna out of the main lobby and into a hallway crowded with a narrow flight of stairs that led to a door which Valerie unlocked with one of a collection of old skeleton keys on a metal ring she kept in her pocket. Inside was an auditorium that spanned the length of the building above the main administration offices. "This is where we occasionally show movies and hold some of our religious services, but for the most part it remains locked." Folding wooden seats were stacked against one wall under a bank of ceiling high cathedral-shaped windows that threw sunlight slanting across the hardwood floor that had been scarred by the passing of more than a century.

Anna followed Valerie quietly to the other side of the room where she unlocked another door that led into a large metal cage that had to be unlocked with yet another heavy skeleton key like a cage at a zoo. Metal mesh lined the railings up to the ceiling to prevent patients from spilling over them. Anna ran her fingertips over the spots where the metal had begun to rust and peel."Just pull that door shut behind you please. It'll lock itself." Anna did as she was asked and tried her best to catch up to Valerie.

The hallways and stairways snaked here and there in an unruly way, first through the newer offices that had been carved out of the administration floors, then through the wards. Anna knew she would never be able to find her way around without help, and she loathed the idea of getting lost in the belly of this beast. Valerie led her down a crooked hallway that ended in another caged staircase with a beautiful turned metal newel post and wrought iron stair fronts. They picked their way past the staircase; there was a tiny green door under the stairs that Valerie told her led to the tunnels and the bowling alley. Rounding the corner Anna found herself in a large day room with bay windows overlooking a courtyard, plastic chairs scattered around haphazardly, an ancient upright piano pushed against a wall.

"Down here there a few wards that have been closed down for a number of years now." They had crossed the threshold, past a rabbit warren of storage closets to a spot where the floor was starting to go soft, the asbestos tiles cracking under their feet. There was a bathroom with two filthy clawfoot tubs, one with its foot sunk nearly through the floor. Doors yawned open and Anna caught sight of sheets of paint hanging from the walls like an advanced case of leprosy giving her a serious case of the creeps. "Needless to say, those wards are strictly off limits. They're dangerous." She pointed to a room off to their right where a couch was beginning to slide towards a crater that had opened up in the middle of the floor like a sinkhole. "The floors are rotting."

By the time Valerie had somehow looped them back to the main lobby, Anna's head spinning and she nearly knocked Valerie over when she stopped to face her.

"That's your tour for now," she finished curtly, then tilted her head to regard her charge. "Can I give you a piece of advice Miss Gilman?" She waited for Anna to nod. "Don't settle in here."

Valerie's bluntness caught her off guard and she stumbled a bit as she followed her to the main doors. "Why is that?"

Sighing, Valerie unbuttoned her blazer then buttoned it again, a nervous habit. "State hospitals are a dying breed." Of course Anna knew that; so many had closed their doors already and there was no end in sight. "This one is most likely next on the chopping block and I'm planning to retire from the Department of Mental Health in a few years. For what it's worth, I think you should do what you came here to do and move on. It's advice I wish I had gotten myself many years ago. "

"Oh." It would have been nice if someone had told her that there was a possibility Westborough might close and she might not be able to finish out her program. "No one told me any of this. Will that affect my internship?"

Valerie shook her head. "It shouldn't. They'll have some sort of plan in place for a gradual phasing down. As for me, I'm sure by then they'll have my replacement waiting in the wings. If they decide to replace me at all." She said it with such a lack of humor that Anna wondered if perhaps she might be more than ready to bid adieu to Westborough.

"How long have you worked here, if you don't mind me asking?"

"I've been here since 1981." Anna immediately noticed that Valerie tensed slightly as she spoke. "I've been with the Department of Mental Health since I graduated from Smith College in 1959. I started out at Northampton State Hospital but came here when the state started pushing for deinstitutionalization and community treatment."

"Wow. So you've seen it all then."

Valerie chuckled sadly. "I most certainly have!" She looked wistful for a moment, lost in some memory that Anna wasn't privy to. "Well, I know it's a lot to take in so why don't you get some dinner, relax a bit, and we'll talk more tomorrow. Questions?"

"About a million. But they can wait." Anna smiled and shook Valerie's hand, then headed out the front door into the late afternoon light that was falling slowly over the asylum, elongating the shadows that nearly touched the banks of the lake. She shaded her eyes from the glow of the setting sun and pulled in the scent of the lake, the burn of the late winter air shooting straight to her head and making her slightly woozy.

"I see you're going to make this whole eyes closed thing a habit." Harper had appeared by her side once again, this time with a white lab coat over her arm.

"I was clearing my head," Anna said, eyes now open, looking out over the lake. "It's peaceful here."

Harper sighed. "The asylum is peaceful. Would that be considered irony?"

Laughing, Anna turned away from the view and squinted at Harper, the setting sun blocking out her profile. "Yes, I suppose it is ironic. But I suppose you learn to take your peace where you can get it."

Chapter 3

When dusk fell Westborough began to look like a city in the midst of a brown out. The front half of the hospital was lit, but just barely, by a single street lamp shining in the direction of the main entrance. An old porch light with a small yellow bulb glowed over the front door of Payne Hall. The back half of the main complex where the wards were already closed was pitch black, the windows like so many blank eyes staring out into the inky night, but Anna couldn't see the main hospital from her room, only the lake, so she sat and watched the water ripple gently in the breeze, wrinkling the moonlight and pushing the shadows from side to side. She had pulled a chair up to her window, propped her feet on the radiator and settled in with a book propped on her lap, but she had been on the same page for the past twenty minutes. She stared out the window instead, her mind wandering back home, back to Buffalo, until a knock on her door brought her around.

Harper was standing outside her room with a bottle of red wine tucked under her arm and two stemmed wine glasses in her hand. "I decided to slum it and sneak into the nurses' quarters for a drinky."

Anna laughed, reaching for the bottle. "I hope you have a corkscrew then. We're not high class enough down here to have our own."

"And *that* is why they put you at the bottom of the hill," she said, pulling a bottle opener out of her pocket. Closing the door behind her, Harper sat on the edge of Anna's bed, tucking her feet under her Indian-style. "How was your ten cent tour with the ice queen?"

Sinking back in her chair, Anna closed her book and tossed it to the floor. Edith Wharton was a favorite of hers but she just couldn't focus. "A blur. I don't think I'll ever be able to find my way around here without a map, or a guide dog."

Harper giggled. "I feel the same. This place is massive and it twists and turns in nonsensical ways. It's enough to make a nun curse."

Anna stared at her then burst out laughing. "That is the greatest thing I have ever heard!" She watched as Harper popped the cork from the wine and artfully poured a glass for each of them without spilling a drop. "Valerie told me today she has been working in state hospitals since 1959. Can you imagine?"

"That's a lifetime," Harper said, giving a mock shiver of horror. "If you think about it, she basically grew up on the wards."

Anna actually hadn't thought about it that way, but now that she considered it, she realized Harper was right. "God. She's us in thirty years."

"A dismal thought."

"And it's all about to come to an end for her."

"What do you mean?" Harper poured herself another glass and took a long pull.

Anna shrugged noncommittally. "She said she's retiring at the end of the year."

"Is that going to affect your internship?"

Shaking her head, Anna swirled her wine in its glass, watching it leave spidery red legs down the sides. "She says it won't. But she also said that I shouldn't put down roots here."

"Why would she say that I wonder." Harper too stared into her glass but Anna noticed her eyes had begun to glaze over. She was two glasses in to Anna's one.

As they finished off the bottle they talked more about their internships. Anna was praying that hers would go smoothly and, in spite of Valerie's advice, hoped the hospital would offer her a full time position when she was finished. She loathed starting over in new places, explaining herself, getting to know people; she preferred to dig in and stay put.

"I think she told me not to settle in because Westborough might be the next to close." She frowned, turning back to the moonlight reflecting off the lake.

Harper, who was now lying diagonally across Anna's skinny twin bed, nodded her head. "I heard the same. There aren't many left in this region. Danvers, Foxboro, Grafton. All gone. I can't imagine Medfield has much longer to go, or even Worcester for that matter."

"And the western part of the state only had Northampton. That's where Valerie came from you know."

"You're fascinated by her, aren't you?" Harper had turned to look at Anna.

"I'm curious about her, that's all," she said, staring at her hands. "I noticed she didn't look me in the eye when she talked about Northampton, not even once."

Harper shrugged. "Can you blame her? I can't imagine it was all roses and champagne. She was there at the height of all of it.

The lobotomies, shock therapy, coma therapy. Christ, she was there for the unholy reign of Thorazine!"

"God, I can't even imagine." Thorazine was powerful enough to sedate a small horse and for a time it was handed out like candy. It was a stop gap, a band aid for overcrowded wards full of actively psychotic patients. "That had to be incredible."

Anna was fascinated by the history of mental health. Her great aunt, her father's sister, had worked at Buffalo State Hospital back home and Anna had eavesdropped on Beatrice whenever she talked about the wards. She had seen photos of porcelain hydrotherapy tubs with their canvas covers, the nurses using giant metal levers to control the water temperature. When she was in high school she had even looked up photos of early lobotomies when they were still performed using ice picks. The graphic images of the ice pick being inserted into the orbital socket were some of the most gruesome she had ever seen, yet she often wished she had been born in another time so she could have sat in the operating theater, watching the Victorian era alienists treat their patients.

She also had a deep and abiding interest in schizophrenia, the most complicated mental illness ever identified. It caused a seemingly random disintegration of the human mind and affected the mind in such a profound way, sometimes splitting in two, or even three, four, five parts until the patient was hearing voices and seeing things. It inspired a fear in her that was almost as powerful as her curiosity, but she told Harper none of this. Instead she listened to Harper's stories of med school dissection pranks and secret society rush parties.

In the small hours of the morning Anna woke with a crick in her neck having fallen asleep sitting up in her chair in front of the window. Harper was still splayed out on the bed, snoring softly. Apparently the wine had worked its magic and knocked them both out; it was 4:00 am according to the clock by the bedside. Anna hobbled stiffly over to the bed and gently pushed Harper over enough so she could climb into bed too, pulling the blankets up over them both, Harper's head sticking out next to Anna's feet. She smiled to herself as she drifted back to sleep. Getting out of bed was going to be mighty difficult.

Chapter 4

Anna and Harper sat together at breakfast, both with fuzzy heads still muddled by too much wine and not enough sleep. Harper was on her third cup of coffee, Anna lagging behind on her second.

"There's not enough caffeine in the world right now," Harper groaned, cradling her head in her hand as she pushed her scrambled eggs around on her plate. "Why did you let me drink that much wine last night?"

"I didn't let you. You were in charge of that bottle," she said, laughing.

"You should have stopped me. You know I can't be trusted with a bottle."

Anna feigned outrage. "And how would I know that Dr. Westcott? I've known you all of five minutes!"

"You're getting a Master's in psychiatric nursing. It's your job to read people."

Shaking her head, Anna gulped down the last of her coffee and stood. "I have to meet with Valerie. Best of luck keeping your eyes open today."

Harper grunted and her head drooped low over her plate. It was going to be a long day for her new friend.

Valerie met Anna at the foot of the main staircase and led her down a narrow hall into an office tucked into the first floor rat maze. The room had no windows and was crowded with filing cabinets, a big metal desk, and a red leather chair that looked wildly out of place amidst the institutional beige of Valerie's office. It had been cut out of a larger room, the walls cheaply cobbled together with drywall and plaster. Anna looked around surreptitiously but realized there was nothing to see—no photographs, no personal items, not even a greeting card tacked to a bulletin board. The office was as sterile as could be. The only thing that identified it as belonging to Valerie Martin was the brass nameplate on her desk.

"Have a seat." Valerie cleared a stack of files off of a large plastic chair that was once yellow, or maybe even cream colored, but was now just drab. It was unlike any other chair Anna had seen before with a deep bucket seat and high molded arms on a fan-shaped back. It was ugly, plain and simple, obviously made to survive a good swift kick or a toss across a day room.

"My apologies for the decor," she said, gesturing toward the chair. "I had a nice, padded green one but a patient ruined it in a fit of pique. So, I assume you've been given paperwork?" Valerie shuffled through the piles on her desk, filing them quickly and efficiently as she questioned Anna.

"Yes, I have it here, I..."

Valerie held up a hand. "Don't bother. You don't need it just yet. The only important thing in that pile is the log for your hours anyway." She continued to move things around until her desktop was clear and Anna could see the calendar beneath which was riddled with appointments and notes scribbled on every available square inch. Finished, Valerie folded her hands on her desk and focused her chilly blue eyes on Anna. "Now, let's talk about your time here."

She went on to explain that it was the first year Westborough had decided to take on psychiatric nursing interns. They were in a hiring freeze, she said, so rather than fighting to bring in new staff who would need transfers when the hospital closed, the administration had voted to utilize interns instead. Anna could tell this annoyed Valerie, that she would rather have staff who were trained and ready to work the wards on their own. She clearly didn't want to babysit Anna who was not allowed on the wards alone.

"Somewhere around here I have a map of the hospital," Valerie added with a smirk. "I saw your face when I was giving you a tour. This place can be tricky for newcomers."

"Did you get lost when you first came here?"

Valerie nodded. "Multiple times. It's not hard to do." She finally laughed. "You should see the tunnel system. It's like *Alice in Wonderland* down there with doors that lead to tunnels that lead to doors that lead to more tunnels. I've taken to writing things on the pipes so I can find my way."

Anna laughed with her at that. She pictured Valerie in the tunnels with a marker, leaving her initials behind like breadcrumbs. "I'm very much looking forward to working alongside you."

Serious again, Valerie sighed. "Be ready for long hours and even longer days. We do a lot around here and we have a little over 800 patients right now. It's roughly a five to one ratio of patients to staff."

Five to one? That was a ridiculous ratio. How were they supposed to provide quality care with that many patients to each nurse?

"The ward staff carry a great deal as well," Valerie said, as if reading Anna's mind. "It's roughly a two to one staff ratio which is the highest it has ever been. We're hoping the department doesn't notice and start taking people away."

"Would they really do that?"

"They would and they have. They're in the process of moving money around. They've already diverted funding from Medfield State Hospital in order to help keep us open."

That funding had gone into shoring up the enormous buildings that were crumbling at an alarming rate. Broken glass littered the floors in the back wards and plaster was crumbling from the walls and ceilings everywhere. The main building was divided up by new, cheap drywall and plywood, makeshift offices carved out in the heart of the original administration building now that one whole wing was unusable; the ceilings on the north side were sagging dangerously. Low, rough carpeting covered the hardwood floors and the remaining tile hallways were chipped and cracked. There was no plan for repairing any of it Valerie said. It was the end of days.

"I assume this is common sense but the closed wards are off limits to patients."

Anna nodded. Those wards gave her the willies.

"We use some of them for storage, mostly furniture, but we still check them regularly. The nurses, not the ward staff."

Lovely. Who would want that task, especially at night? "Why don't they seal them off?"

Valerie shrugged. "No idea. It's a department decision in which we have little input if I'm being honest. They don't realize what a hazard those things are."

Or how unsettling. "I guess if you have to do it, you have to do it. I suppose there's no arguing with the state."

"Not at all. Bureaucracies rarely see sense."

Anna sat back in the horrid yellow chair. "I can see that."

"Why don't we get started? I'll take you up and introduce you to some of the patients." Valerie stood and led Anna up the main staircase, back through the auditorium and into the wards. They were sunny and clean but they showed their age, the paint beginning to peel where the walls met the ceiling. The wood floors were freshly waxed but some of the planks had begun to lift and twist, turning the hallway into an obstacle course and Anna watched the other nurses tiptoe across the floors, knowing exactly where to step. The nurses' station was just a smaller version of the patients' rooms with a Dutch door and kitchen cabinets hung on one wall. A small round table was pushed in the corner with two mismatched chairs, the top crowded with magazines and old Avon catalogs.

Anna trailed after Valerie as she named off the patients in each room; she thought how grateful she was that their names were stuck to each of the doors giving her a fifty-fifty shot of getting them right. Almost every room was full, each with two beds, sometimes three if there was enough space and there was no superfluous furniture anywhere.

"Valerie, if there are so many patients, why did they close the back wards? Why not repair them instead?"

Valerie glanced over her shoulder as she led Anna to the next room where a woman sat on the edge of her bed, staring out the window. Anna could see that her line of sight took her right to the lake. "Like I said earlier, funding."

"But you said funding was being diverted from Medfield to make repairs here."

"They did make repairs. Mostly to the administration building, the one place the public actually sees on a semi-regular basis."

Anna shook her head, not necessarily shocked but certainly disgusted by the lack of foresight. "Those back wards are an eyesore, and these ones are overcrowded."

Chuckling, Valerie stopped and put her hand on Anna's shoulder. "Now you see why I told you not to settle in here. You think these decisions would be based in common sense, but instead they wear you down with their constant *lack* of sense."

So instead she would have Anna move on to another hospital, maybe even another field? Was that what Valerie was getting at? "I just think this place could offer so much more if things were different."

"That's how I felt when I first started a hundred years ago," Valerie said, leading Anna back to the nurses' station. "Eventually that idealism drifts away."

"How disappointing."

Valerie shrugged. "It broke my heart when it happened to me." She shook her head, then changed the subject. "Let me show you where all the logs are kept."

Anna wondered, not for the first time, what had happened to Valerie Martin at Northampton State Hospital. It was obvious that whatever it was, it was serious enough to have turned her into this jaded, no-nonsense "ice queen" as Harper called her. She could tell that Valerie had once loved her job but now she talked of the hospital in a rather clinically detached manner that suggested she had checked out of her job a long time ago, but Anna suspected that it was more than just the job alone that had broken Valerie's heart.

Chapter 5

However bleak Valerie's prognosis was for the hospital, Anna's first months at Westborough passed quickly and she fell into a routine. The cold winds of late winter gave way to the teasing warmth of early spring; the leaves came back to the trees and the corn fields began to grow again, new spikes pushing through the earth and reaching for the sun. By summer the buildings were sweltering, the wards clammy with humidity but Anna had survived and was finding enjoyment in the hospital library; she had discovered a collection of volumes on the history of asylums that caught her fancy and she spent all her free time sitting on the floor, her back against the stacks, reading.

To her surprise Valerie had been more than willing to talk about Northampton, as far as the daily operations were concerned anyway. She told Anna stories about life on the wards in the 1960's, the advances in treatment, and the changes she helped to bring to the wards, but Anna noticed that no matter how much she shared,she never mentioned any patients by name and she never talked about any friends or family. Sometimes Anna would ask questions, try to draw more out of her, but Valerie was tight-lipped. She never slipped up, never mentioned something by accident or started a sentence only to stop in the middle. She could see that Valerie was good at keeping secrets.

One afternoon, as Anna sat on the banks of the Chauncy reading an ancient book on mental health policy, Harper skipped across the gravel road and dropped a folded plaid blanket next to her, flopping down on it and stretching her legs out in front of her. "How goes the reading?"

Sighing, Anna closed the book and tossed it onto the grass. She leaned back and turned her face to the sky but it was difficult not to let a tiny smile creep onto her face.

"I'm beginning to think you're on a mission to get through every book in that library" Harper playfully slapped her on the arm and shook her head. "You're developing an obsession."

Anna threw a look over her shoulder and laughed. "I'm not obsessed. I just find it all so fascinating."

They reclined on the grass, watching the Canadian geese strutting along the shore while puffy white clouds lazed around in the sky. "Have you found any interesting patients yet?" she asked, turning to look at Harper.

Shrugging, Harper reached into her pocket and pulled out a pack of cigarettes. "Honestly, not yet. But I've only met a few of them, mostly nervous cases." She pulled a cigarette out of the pack and lit it, then offered them to Anna who shook her head. "Oh, so you're one of those are you." Inhaling deeply, Harper blew the smoke up into the tree branches in little rings.

"I am not 'one of those'. I just don't share your love of ingesting copious amounts of nicotine on top of gallons of coffee a day."

"That's because you're not a medical intern. The rest of you lot have it easy." She reached out and swatted Anna on the shoulder, laughing. Harper had absolute respect for Anna but loved to tease her about her just the same. Anna liked to think the humor humbled Harper and made Anna feel like she was on par with her friend.

"I was hoping there might be more complex cases I could observe. Schizophrenia, maybe."

Anna sat up a little straighter and let herself go rigid. "Schizophrenia?"

"Yes," Harper exhaled. "It's a fascinating mental illness. The mind essentially destroys itself and no one knows why."

Anna knew why. It destroyed itself because it couldn't process what was happening around it, but she didn't say that. She let Harper talk about her clinical experiences with schizophrenia patients but her mind was elsewhere, at her childhood home in Buffalo where she could still hear the slamming of doors and the whispers of concerned adults huddled outside doors.

"Hey, are you even listening to me?" Harper was snapping her fingers in front of Anna's face, trying to get her attention.

"What? Oh sorry. I was somewhere else."

"Yes, I could see that. Want to tell me where?"

Anna shook her head. "It's nothing. I was just thinking."

Harper rolled her eyes and folded her arms behind her head, crossing her ankles and settling in. " Well go on then, go back to your reading. I'm going to take a nap."

"Don't stay out here too long. The geese might mistake you for bread." Anna gathered up her book and the sweater she had been sitting on and headed back to the dorm. She tossed the book on the ever growing pile and picked up a novel instead, but she couldn't focus. She rolled over on her back and tented the book on her chest, closing her eyes. Sometimes she dreamed about that house in Buffalo with the hardwood floors that always rang with the sound of anxious footfalls and the clanging of the doorbell. Anna spent most of her childhood retreating into books like *Anne of Green Gables* and *The Secret Garden*, stories where children who had less than desirable circumstances somehow found their way in the world. They were her only escape from the strange reality that surrounded her.

Finally she was able to leave for college, from Buffalo to Massachusetts, but she couldn't escape the memories— the hushed voice, the muffled footsteps. It was the end of her first break from school when her mother died. After the funeral she remembered going to her bedroom and sitting on the bed she hadn't slept in for months, staring out the window. A snow storm had descended and she watched as the trees filled with snow, lost in her thoughts for what seemed like hours while the house filled with relatives, some of whom Anna had never even met. Not once did her father come to her or try to comfort her. Even as they stood in the church, Anna's eyes fixed on her mother's coffin under a shroud of flowers, her father stood as far apart from her as he could without actually leaving their pew. When the service was over and the final procession began, Anna felt herself growing dizzy and she started to sway but her father didn't notice, or perhaps didn't care. Instead it was her Aunt Sarah who put a hand out to steady her niece and guide her down the aisle. It was a relief when the break ended and Anna was able to put hundreds of miles between herself and that house of horrors she had once called home. All that she took with her this time were her books and a ring that had belonged to her mother-- a silver and onyx mourning ring. She left everything else behind.

Fall descended on the asylum as Anna and Valerie forged something of a bond, working side by side each day and talking about everything under the sun. She told Valerie bits and pieces about her life in Buffalo, her years at UMASS; Valerie had graduated from Smith and told Anna she had wanted to be a writer once upon a time but that life had had other plans for her.

Anna wished she had some talent when it came to writing. She loved literature and she loved to read but writing just wasn't in her blood. Valerie on the other hand had shelves in her office that were filled with the leather bound journals she had spent years filling with words and sketches, stories about her life, her patients, her coworkers.

Sometimes Anna would sit in Valerie's office, staring at those cracked leather spines with the yellow ribbon bookmarks, and she would feel curiosity crushing her, her fingers itching to slide one of those slim volumes off the top shelf and page through it, read all of Valerie's secrets.

Once she caught Anna staring at the books. "Maybe you should consider keeping a journal."

She shrugged. What would she write about?

"Write about your day, your thoughts, your feelings. Words that sound good to you, snippets of interesting conversation."

"But I'm not really much of a writer."

"Writing is a process, not a product," Valerie said, pulling a brand new journal out of her desk. "Even a grocery list is writing if you're putting pen to paper. It's therapeutic." She pressed the journal into Anna's hand and ushered her out of the office. "Go. Write. Get to know yourself."

Chapter 6

The patient census was still high, while rumors about closure continued to swirl. Anna and Harper tried not to discuss it; instead they read together and sunned themselves down at the lake while the rest of the hospital crumbled around them. They were just beginning to feel as if things were well in hand when they got notice that a group of patients would be transferring in from Medfield.

"Where the hell are we going to put more patients?" Harper stood in the day room, waving a lit cigarette as she gestured at the hallways that were beginning to feel mighty crowded.

Anna sat at a table with a printed map of the wards in front of her, trying to figure out how to rearrange the rooms to add more beds. "I honestly don't know Dr. Impatient. I'm trying to figure out how to help you right now and your nagging isn't helping."

"I'm sorry but no matter how I puzzle it out we can't possibly fit more patients in here."

Turning her hand drawn map sideways, Anna erased one bed and moved it to another room, writing a patient name across it, then held it up to look it over one last time. "Yes we can. Here." She handed it to Harper and waited as she looked at each of her carefully sketched out room assignments.

"Oh my God. You're a genius Gilman."

"Why thank you Westcott." Anna took the map back from her and shook off the eraser shavings. "Now all you have to do is put it into action and hope that nothing goes wrong."

Harper picked up the phone and called the nursing supervisors to the day room. Valerie, along with a small harried woman named Celeste, gave Anna's drawing a cursory glance, declared it acceptable and got the move started. Valerie and Celeste went from room to room, letting the patients know they would have to pack their things and be ready to make some adjustments. Some complained a bit, distress evident on their faces, but overall the move went smoothly and the staff worked well into the night dragging beds into the emptied rooms, readying them for the new residents. Anna helped the patients remake their beds and hang their things in their new closets. She collected books and stray shoes, trying to match them to their owners.

When the day came, Anna stood close to Harper stood shoulder on the front porch waiting for the van that would bring ten new patients from Medfield State Hospital. She watched as each one was led out of the vehicle and up the stairs to where the medical staff waited for them. Anna counted seven females and three males; it was well known that females were statistically more likely to get committed than males, though these days it was no longer a matter of women being committed by bored or jealous husbands. Females were more likely to seek help when depression got the better of them, more likely to talk freely about their feelings and struggles. Men generally tried to tough it out; those who ended up hospitalized were desperate.

"This one," Harper whispered, pointing to one of the patients. "Paranoid schizophrenic. Watch yourself with that one."

His name was Peder Roderick and he had been a literature professor at Boston University. He was young, only thirty five, but he had been in and out of hospitals since he was in his teens. Somehow he had managed to finish his college degree and hold down a job for almost three years before his symptoms began to get the better of him. It seemed his medication was no longer working and he began hallucinating while quoting Chaucer, peppering his lectures with obscenities directed at enemies only he could see. One afternoon as he was teaching a lesson on Proust, he began to sweat profusely and couldn't seem to remember what he was saying. As he moved toward the lectern he muttered something about a glass of water and collapsed.

According to his file, he had been taken to Boston Psychopathic for observation. When it was determined that his condition had progressed beyond the reaches of the usual treatment, he was packed off to Medfield and now to Westborough. Anna watched the line of patients go by, scrutinizing each of them as they came off the van. Peder Roderick looked up and caught Anna staring, his green eyes locking with hers. She quickly looked away but she could feel her face flush with warmth and she watched him carefully from the corner of her eye.

Anna couldn't help but notice that he was unusually handsome and still well-kept for a patient on a psych ward. His brown hair was neatly combed, his beard trimmed and smoothed. He held his head high and his shoulders back, walking carefully and purposefully, a stark contrast to the medicated shuffle of the other patients. His eyes held hers as he took each step in a deliberate manner, brushing past her as he was led through the front door. As his elbow brushed against hers she felt a jolt like lightning skipping up her spine.

"Are you ok?" Harper leaned over and whispered in her ear.

Anna swallowed and tried to look casual. "Of course. Why?"

"You have the strangest look on your face." Harper glanced over her shoulder at the new patients, then followed the group into the lobby leaving Anna to close and bolt the doors behind them. With her back to everyone, Anna took her time locking the doors, closing her eyes and taking a deep breath. She looked down at her shaking hands, embarrassed that she had allowed Peder Roderick to unnerve her so and she suddenly felt very silly. Shaking her head she turned to head upstairs. As she came around the corner into the day room, Anna hung back and caught sight of Peder Roderick. She watched him take in every bit of his surroundings, nodding politely to everyone who passed him, yet with a stiffness that put distance between him and the others. He was tall, lithe, and strong, and as he looked around Anna could see the muscles in his jaw working, his hands clenching then stretching at his side; she wondered if it was a sign of anxiety or of strength.

"You have that look on your face again." Harper was standing in the door to the break room, leaning against the jamb while she lit a cigarette. "What gives Gilman?"

"Peder Roderick, there's something about the way he looks at me." She shrugged and smiled as if amused by her own paranoia. "It's nothing. I'm just being strange."

"Now you see what I said to stay away from him. He's handsome, but dangerous."

"Oh," she said quietly. "Has he ever hurt anyone?"

Harper nodded. "But I won't give you the gory details. He's an interesting case though, having been able to hold down a job, blend in, for so long before needing to be hospitalized."

"Was he ever married?"

Harper gave her a sharp look. "Odd question. But no, never married, no children." She took a drag of her cigarette and flicked the ash in the metal bin behind her. "I wouldn't think too deeply on that one if I was you."

"I just wondered what he was like. You know, before."

"A psychotic break is loud, messy. He was hearing voices and likely hallucinating for quite some time before he landed himself in the hospital. He was on the violent ward for a time when he was at Medfield."

"That does sound messy. Do you know what kind of visions he has?" Anna had learned from the books that she had read that schizophrenia, like all mental illnesses, manifested itself differently in each human being and she always wondered what fueled each patient's individual delusions. The most common were religious ones—the street prophets who believed they were the second coming of Christ and went around declaring that the end was nigh. Then there were those who became rabid government conspiracy theorists, claiming they were being followed by the CIA or wanted by the FBI.

"He has apocalyptic visions. Death. Doom and gloom. That sort of thing. Says he sees the 'blackness that hides in the human soul'. Scary stuff."

The hair on her arms stood up and she wondered why he had picked her out of the crowd, making direct eye contact with her and no one else. Thinking about it frightened her.

"You have that look on your face again."

Anna looked up at Harper. "What look?"

"Thunderstruck. Like someone is setting fire to the soles of your feet."

She shook her head again. "No, I'm fine. I was just somewhere else."

Anna went down to the ward kitchen to see if she could scare up a cup of tea and a cookie or two. She carried the cup, cookies, and her sweater back to her room and settled in to read for a few hours. Then she pulled out the journal Valerie had gotten her and fished in her desk for a pen. Anna had always found it hard to write, harder still to write about herself in any serious way, so instead of fighting to fill the blank pages with anything meaningful, she began to record everything she had done that day, including the moment she met Peder Roderick. She polished off her cookies as she wrote detailed entries that spanned every fifteen minutes for the entire eleven hours she had been awake, her tea growing cold in her other hand. By the time she had finished, her hand was cramped and the sun was setting. Looking at the clock she realized she had passed so much time that it she would need to hurry if she wanted to eat.

Dinner was served in the main cafeteria at the rear of the campus, a great, green room with soaring ceilings. The floor was a U shape that crowded around a central serving area, double doors on the right hiding the massive kitchens filled with steel, industrial-sized appliances that held and made enough food for the more than 10,000 patients. Grabbing a tray and piling it with steaming plates of food, Anna threaded her way through the tables and found one by the windows. The cafeteria overlooked a small courtyard that bordered the older wards, the ones that were no longer in operation. and one of the windows was open slightly, letting in a waft of chill mid-winter air. She leaned her shoulder against the concrete sill and stared out for a moment; a sudden movement across the way caught her eye and made her jump. She looked up just in time to see a curtain moving in an upper floor window of the old ward, as if someone had been holding it open and quickly let it fall back in place.

She jumped like a frightened cat when Harper dropped her tray on the table next to her and sat down. "What's the deal there twitchy?"

Hurrying back to the ward, Anna searched for Celeste and found her in a patient's room. "Is there someone doing checks? Are they running late?"

"I... I think I just saw someone in one of the windows in the old ward."

"Someone's probably just up there doing checks." Harper shrugged it off and picked at her salad. "I wouldn't worry about it."

Anna looked up, waiting for the curtain to move again but there was no sign that anyone was there. "I must be losing my mind." She took one last look across the courtyard and was about to take her tray up when she noticed something on the window. The curtain had fallen back in place but not quite all the way. She squinted hard and saw what looked like a small smudgy handprint on the otherwise clear window. She blinked again and it was gone.

Chapter 7

The next time Anna saw Peder Roderick he was outside helping tend the greenhouse. Spring was on its way and shades of green had begun to creep back over the campus. Peder was bent over a tray of seedlings, delicately transferring them from the tray to the palettes that served as tables in the greenhouse closest to the hospital. She was taking a walk around the campus and the path around the greenhouse was the last leg of her walk, coming up from the path that followed the perimeter of the lake and wound back up to the main administration hall. As she passed, Peder looked up, his hands still busy with the plans, watching her as she came up the hill. Stopping to chat with Fitz, the red-headed twenty-something who supervised the patients in the greenhouse and garden, Anna stole glimpses of Peder from the corner of her eye. Fitz caught her looking and jerked his thumb in Peder's direction.

"Here, let me introduce you to the new guys." He took her by the elbow and led her over to an older gentleman in a wheelchair sat with a pot of begonias in his lap. "This is Mr. Halworth. Say hello Mr. Halworth!" Fitz had raised his voice substantially and still Mr. Halworth seemed not to hear him. Whispering an aside to Anna he said, "Deaf as a post that one."

On the other end of the greenhouse was a middle aged man who could only be described as utterly nondescript. He was up to his elbows in a bag of mulch but it looked as if he had forgotten what he was supposed to be doing with it. "That's Mr. McCray. He doesn't speak, doesn't make eye contact, but I've found he loves to stick his hands in the mulch. Doesn't do anything with it besides dig his hands in there but it seems to keep him calm."

Anna watched the man's facial expressions change as he drew his hands out of the bag, looked at them covered in black mulch, then plunged them back in. She thought she saw a hint of a smile as he flexed his fingers and dirt flaked off, falling to the ground around him, but she probably imagined it. He was simply transfixed by the entire process, repeating it over and over; in reality there wasn't much more connection than that.

At last Fitz led her over to Peder who watched her approach like a curious animal. He took one last seedling off the tray and placed it gently on the palette, wiping his hands off on his hospital issue pants.

"I'm Peder Roderick," he said, putting his hand out for Anna to shake.

"Pleasure to meet you." Anna dropped her eyes in discomfort as Peder took in every bit of her face, her cheeks aflame with embarrassment as he was clearly assessing her. He held her hand just a moment too long, her skin hot under his touch. Part of her wanted to rip her hand from his, but something inside of her thrilled at his touch. When he finally did let go of her hand, she noticed the distinct absence of Peder's warmth.

Embarrassed, she turned and strode quickly away, calling over her shoulder, "It was a pleasure to meet you all." Her heart was racing and she felt if Peder could somehow see right through to her insides, tied in knots as she forced one foot in front of the other.

Peder was magnetic but he was also mentally ill, and regardless of how charming or "normal" a patient may seem, it would be a mistake to believe the charade. Anna had to accept that Peder could easily lead her to fall under that spell of charm and purported normalcy; he looked like many of the young men Anna had encountered on campus wearing tweeds and discussing literature or asking girls out to parties, except that instead he was wearing hospital grays and was heavily medicated.

That evening Anna was in the cafeteria, sitting at a table with a book in her hand. It was a worn, leather bound copy of *Ethan Frome* that she had found in the library. Frankly the book was boring her to tears but she was hesitant to admit defeat.

"How do you like it?"

"Pardon?" She looked up to find that Peder Roderick had materialized next to her table.

"The book," he said. "I've read it a number of times."

"Honestly I'm having a hard time making it through the first time let alone multiple readings." Anna shifted in her seat and tried not to look at him. She couldn't get over the color of his eyes-- the exact shade of green of a carefully polished emerald offset by lashes that would make any woman jealous. His skin was tan, much darker than hers, making her wonder what his nationality might be, and she could see that he was fit, toned-- but still. "Dr. Westcott told me you were...are a literature professor?"

He sat down and settled him across from Anna, making it difficult for her to avoid making eye contact with him. "I was. At Boston University. Modern American Literature."

"That's wonderful," she said, trying to keep her tone cool and only politely interested. "I can't even imagine. I love to read but it must be something else to teach a room full of students."

"It is." He reached out and tapped the cover of the book, the vibration moving through the leather and up her arms. "I love books and words and stories. The only fault I could ever find with teaching was the moment when I could see that a student just wasn't connecting to a book that had moved me tremendously."

As he talked, Anna carefully watched his eyes almost change color as he spoke, the emotion of speaking about literature welling up as he talked. He told her how much he loved the classics-- *The Great Gatsby, Heart of Darkness, The House of Mirth*. Wharton was a particular favorite of his and the corners of his lips turned up slightly when he talked about having once visited her home in Lenox. "The Berkshires are beautiful. It's easy to see why she chose The Mount as her home." He was masculine and enigmatic, but Anna consciously reminded herself that he had once been considered violent.

"I've never been."

Peder smiled broadly at her, a dazzling sight that lit up his whole face and sped the nervous beat of Anna's heart. "You should go. It's incredible. Perhaps one day I'll…" He trailed off as if remembering where he was and why he was there, having this conversation in an asylum cafeteria rather than in a lecture hall. "At any rate, it's worth the drive," he finished quietly, looking down at his hands.

"Then I'll add it to my list."

"Are you from the area?"

Anna frowned. She didn't feel right answering personal questions from him but she also felt she couldn't be blatantly rude. "Buffalo originally."

"I visited Buffalo once. Niagara Falls for a family vacation about a hundred years ago."

Peder said he was a Massachusetts native and Anna learned quickly that he possessed, and liked to share, an almost encyclopedic knowledge of its history, both literary and otherwise. She sat and listened to him talk, his voice like velvet, and she silently admitted that part of her could have listened to him go on like that for hours. He told her about Thoreau's Walden Pond and the bridge where the American Revolution began. He believed in ghosts and knew where every historic haunt was located and knew more about the asylum system in New England than Anna could ever have learned from the books she read. She drew herself up short when she remembered that was because he had been committed so many times. Frowning, she glanced at her watch and feigned distress, as if she had somewhere urgent to be.

"I'm keeping you," he said, gesturing toward her watch.

"Well, yes actually. I have to be getting back." She stood and smoothed down her skirt of sorry that she had drawn his gaze to that region of her body. "Have a nice evening Mr. Roderick."

"Please, call me Peder," he said, standing as well. "And it was my pleasure."

"Peder then. Enjoy your evening." Anna turned and walked away as quick as she could, leaving Peder to his meal without her.

The next evening Harper appeared shortly before dinner to see if Anna wanted to go down to the cafeteria. "I hear it's roast beef tonight. Not sure if that's roast beef as we know it or some bizarre bastardization of it. Might be worth a look though."

"Sure I could use a break." Her stomach growled; she hadn't bothered with lunch, nor had she seen Harper all day. She yawned and stretched, her mouth dry and sticky. "And I need something to drink."

Harper snorted. "If only."

"I meant a soda you lush." They walked down to the kitchen , the aroma of beef cooking wafting from the open doors. As they headed for the line, Anna caught sight of Peder sitting at the same table as she had been the previous evening with a book in his hand that looked to be another of Edith Wharton's creations. He looked up and caught her eye, nodding almost imperceptibly with a hint of a smile.

She felt herself flush and turned away to find that Harper was watching her with an amused smile. "Are you alright?"

"What? Yes. I'm fine. It's a bit warm in here, isn't it?" Anna fanned herself, pretending to be overheated.

"A likely story. I saw you looking at Peder Roderick. He gets under your skin doesn't he." Harper peered over Anna's head to where Peder had returned to his reading. "Rest easy. There's nothing to fear. We have him under close watch."

Harper thought she was afraid of him? "Oh, well yes. Of course you do."

"Look, I can see it on your face. You're terrified of him. In fact you've broken out in hives."

Anna looked down to see angry red splotches spreading across her chest, her skin hot to the touch. "My God, I have. I'm a mess."

"Yes, you are. But you're in the right place. Now stop worrying about our Mr. Roderick and let's go eat."

Chapter 8

One evening, once spring had well and truly settled in and there were buds on the trees, Anna found herself in the day room, sweeping up the first wisps of pollen that had collected on the floor. Each massive frame in the expansive bay window was twice the size of a normal one in both height and width. They opened like a normal double hung window, except with the aid of a key, and the screens had been replaced with heavy metal mesh, rows of tiny silver diamonds just large enough for a patient to fit their fingertips in, but no more than that.

They had received six more patients from Medfield and two from Worcester State Hospital with the promise of more on the way in the coming months which made Anna wonder if

Valerie's assessment of Westborough's future had missed its mark as they were now stretched to the gills. She secretly hoped this was a sign that things were turning around because she had grown quite attached to the place, though she couldn't imagine what that said about her that she had found comfort in an aging insane asylum.

Smiling to herself, she swept the yellow fluff into a pile and pushed it into the dustpan, walking it over to the bin. She pulled the chain on the light in the broom closet so she could see the nail the broom belonged on. As she returned the broom to its spot she heard someone running down the hall. Poking her head around the corner she saw one of the nurses, Alice Lambert, barreling headlong down the hallway.

"Nurse Lambert, what's going on?" Anna hastily backed out of the broom closet and shut the door behind her.

"It's Peder. Peder Roderick isn't in his room." She was breathing hard from running and could barely get the words out. "He's done this once before. Last time we found him in the old wing. I have to call Valerie."

"You go ahead and sit, catch your breath." Anna pulled up a chair and pushed Alice into it. "Call Valerie. I'll go look for him."

"No Anna! We have to wait for Valerie!" She shouted, as Anna took off in the direction of the men's' ward. "It's not your..." but Anna was gone.

The power to the old halls had been cut off to save money, the heating disconnected as well, and as dusk descended a chill night breeze shot in through the broken windows and cooled the stone walls. Anna picked her way carefully across the floors, quickly peeking into rooms along the way, calling Peder's name softly as if she might disturb someone. She glanced into each room as she went but there was no sign of him anywhere.

Then at the end of the hall she came to the room where she had seen the handprint on the glass pane, the room where she thought she had seen something in the window. When she looked inside she found Peder standing motionless, staring out over the courtyard.

"Peder, what are you doing in here?" She whispered but he didn't respond, didn't even acknowledge that she was there. "Peder?" Moving slowly, Anna crept up behind him and looked out over his shoulder to see what he was so focused on but all she saw was the lengthening shadows of the coming night. She reached out and tapped him on the shoulder, and though he turned to look at her, his eyes were glassy and unfocused, as if he was actually looking through her rather than at her.

He was in a trance of some sort; Anna was afraid to bring him out of it so she simply waited. Peder turned his attention back to the window and leaned forward, pressing his forehead to the glass, rocking it back and forth. He began to moan, softly at first, then louder until Anna realized he was saying, "no, no, no" over and over.

He was beginning to frighten her and she wanted nothing more than to get out of that room so she clapped her hands in front of his face and yelled, "Peder, Peder. Snap out of it!" The room was lit softly by the light of the moon as it rose in the sky, the walls and floor glowing in the white light. She grabbed Peder and shook him until his eyes finally focused. "Peder, what are you doing in here?"

Confusion clouded his face as he looked around the room, trying to figure out where he was. "Miss Gilman?"

"Yes, it's me. It's Anna."

"Where am I?"

"You're in the old wing, in a patient room"

He looked around again, taking in the peeling painted walls, the cracked tile floors, and the torn curtains. "I shouldn't be here."

"No you shouldn't," she said sternly, then seeing the look of confusion in his eyes, softened her tone. "Let's get you back to the ward." Anna reached down and took Peder's elbow, leading him back to his room. Sitting him down on his bed, Anna pulled up a chair as Peder lay down and settled himself on his pillow, staring up at his ceiling.

"Nurse Lambert told me this isn't the first time this has happened."

Sighing, he closed his eyes and shook his head. "No, it isn't. I sleep walk, have done all my life."

"Do you remember getting out of bed?"

He shook his head again and grimaced. "I don't. I never remember any of it. I don't know how I got there, or why I was in that room, but this is the second time I've ended up in that room."

"Always that room?'

Peder nodded. "The first time I went there was my very first night on the wards. One of the orderlies said he watched me climb out of bed and head straight for that hallway, for that room, as if I knew exactly where I was going."

Anna sat back in the chair and brought her hand to her chin as she considered what he was saying. Something about that room was drawing him there, something powerful enough to lure him, every night, deep in sleep, to that same window where Anna swore she had seen someone, the handprint that had been left behind by some invisible hand.

"I saw something in that room once." She said quietly. "I was in the cafeteria not too long ago and I happened to look up at those wards. I could swear I saw the curtains move, maybe hand. Does that sound ridiculous?"

"No," Peder said. "It's not ridiculous at all when you think of how many people have probably stood at that window over the years. This hospital has been in operation for more than a century."

"I never thought of it that way."

"And imagine how many of them have died here in hospital." He said it the way the British did, *in hospital*.

"So you think that I did see someone, and that it might have been a spirit or something?"

Peder shrugged. "It's possible."

"Do you believe in that sort of thing?" Anna had never been the kind of person who gave much thought to ghosts or spirits, the afterlife. In fact the idea of life after death frightened her so much that she actually hoped life simply ended after taking that final breath because she couldn't imagine it all dragging out much more.

"Actually, I do." Peder moved his thumb slowly in circles on the back of Anna's hand, an intimate gesture that both comforted and unnerved her further. "Maybe I read too much, but I think maybe someone or something was trying to get your attention."

Anna scoffed. "I doubt that. I'm sure it was just a breeze."

"Don't be so quick to dismiss the possibilities. There's an energy in that room, didn't you feel it when you were in there?"

"No, I didn't. That's a load of garbage."

He shrugged again. "Who knows but it wasn't coincidence that you were drawn to look up at that window. Whatever pricked your subconscious, I believe it's the same thing that draws me there in the middle of the night."

Chapter 9

The next morning at breakfast Anna mentioned Peder's nocturnal wanderings to Harper who immediately put it down to his illness; sleep walking wasn't uncommon in schizophrenics and his assertion that there was something drawing him to the back wards made sense considering the visions he had been having since he was a child.

"According to his parents he kept wandering off in the middle of the night and they would find him out in the fields behind their house just staring," Harper said, vigorously salting her eggs. "For months he maintained that he couldn't remember how he got outside or why he was in the fields, but that something had lead him out there."

"He said the same thing about that room."

Harper shrugged. "It's just the ramblings of a diseased mind. Don't let it get to you. Don't let *him* get to you."

"I'm trying not to but there's something about him, something that's just sticking in the back of mind that I can't quite put my finger on."

"I'm sure it's just your subconscious overreacting. Don't sweat it."

Anna shrugged and took a bite of her English muffin. She and Harper made it a point to eat breakfast together every day, talking and laughing together, Anna commiserating with Harper who had acquired a few very testy patients. For the rest of the meal she tried not to belabor the subject of Peder Roderick but she couldn't stop thinking about him and though Harper was relentless in reminding her that Peder was not only mentally ill, but also dangerous, it was too late-- he had gotten into Anna's head.

What troubled her most about everything Peder had said was the suggestion that there might be a spirit in that room. Slipping off to the library, Anna quietly wandered the stacks searching for books about ghosts, hauntings, the afterlife. Each time she found one, she added it to a pile she had started in the far corner out of sight of the rest of the room, and when she was satisfied that she had a broad enough selection, she sat down with her back against the radiator and began turning pages. She flipped past images of witches being hanged, seances being held in Victorian parlors, ghosts appearing in photographs with their loved ones. She found it hard to believe just how strongly so many people bought into the idea of hauntings.

What she found most interesting was a story about two sisters from New York, Maggie and Kate Fox who woke one night to the sound of knocking in their bedroom. After a lengthy search, the girls' father could find no explanation for the knocking, though it repeated itself each night. Finally Maggie and Kate devised a system for communicating with the ghostly knocker by asking it questions and allowing it to answer with different patterns of knocks. They claimed the spirit told them he was murdered in that very house and buried in the basement, but there was no body, no evidence of a murder.

Though no one could identify the source of the knocks, many of their contemporaries firmly believed that the sounds were genuine spirit activity and the Fox sisters went on tour, demonstrating their ability to communicate with the dead. Dropping the book in her lap, Anna leaned into the warmth of the radiator and closed her eyes. Could the dead really communicate? Could that be what the handprint on the window was all about?

She shook her head and laughed at herself, at the naive notion that there was a spirit in that room that was trying to get her attention.

Anna got up and stretched, her legs stiff from sitting on the floor, and went to reshelve the books, but she couldn't bring herself to put away the book about the Fox sisters. There was no harm in taking the book back to her room and finishing it. Maybe it would help her understand why Peder felt so strongly that there was something paranormal happening in that room. Tucking the book under her arm, Anna hurried back to her room and tucked the book away in her top drawer alongside her journal.

That night, as a thunderstorm rolled in over the lake, Anna went around closing the windows in the day room only to be interrupted by a breathless young nurse hurrying down the hall, one of the new girls whose name Anna could never remember. Beatrice? Barbara? Brittany?

"He's done it again," she heard the girl say to Nurse Lambert. "He's not in his room and I have no idea where he could be."

Anna knew they were talking about Peder and she immediately set off for the back wards. She walked quickly, knowing exactly where to put her feet to avoid the soft spots in the floor, though she trailed one hand along the wall to guide her. Without even bothering to look in the other rooms, she headed straight for the end of the hall and the room on the right. There he was, his forehead pressed against the window and as Anna approached, Peder lifted his hand and held it just inches away from the glass. She stood next to him and leaned in to look closer; she saw that his fingers were poised above a thin, delicate handprint, slightly smudged around the edges, that had appeared on the window pane. Looking around her she could see that there were no other footprints in the dust, only hers and Peder's; no one else had been in the room yet the handprint was there, clear as day.

She reached down and took Peder roughly by the elbow and led him back to his room, sitting in silence with him until his eyes focused and he regained his grasp on reality. She was grateful that this time he didn't seem to want to talk, he just sat, staring at the ceiling until he drifted off to sleep. For a few minutes she sat in the near darkness watching him sleep. The thing about an asylum was that no room was ever completely dark. Lights out was a bit of a misnomer since every third light actually stayed on throughout the night. In the half light, or one third light she supposed, she could see the fine lines around his eyes and in the corners of his mouth. She figured he was at least ten years older than she, maybe even more, but in sleep he looked so young, so normal. Pushing her chair back, she lingered a moment more before leaving to tell Valerie that Peder was safe in his room, then went to empty the trash bins in the dumpster out back.

Anna took the back stairs and ducked out the side door into the courtyard outside the cafeteria. She dragged the cans halfway to the gate and stopped just inside it to look up at the window. It was dark and though she was squinting hard, she saw no movement; the curtain was still, the window black. She kept walking toward the maintenance building but a flurry of motion caught her eye and made her look up again just as the curtain parted and a hand appeared at the glass, clear as day. Anna gasped and took a step back, bumping against the stone wall behind her. Her knees buckled under her and she tumbled backward, landing hard on the paved path that led out of the courtyard.

For a moment Anna lay on the ground and looked up at the sky, assessing whether or not she had broken anything but it seemed she had just knocked the wind out of herself. Sitting up, she dusted herself off and checked each elbow, both skinned raw from hitting the asphalt, blood seeping down her arm. Her clothes were ruined, caked in dirt, her jeans torn at the knees and her hair untangled from its tie. She looked up at the window a second time but now the curtain was back in place, blank and motionless once again.

Shaking herself off, Anna gingerly dragged the bins the rest of the way, emptying them in the dumpster outside the maintenance building. The sticky summer air made her elbows sting and her head started to spin, a headache creeping up behind her eyes. Stowing the empty bins in their alcove on the ward, she went to the nurses' station and tended to her elbows, cleaning them and dressing them with gauze, then returned to her room and fell heavily into bed, not even bothering to change her clothes. In moments she was asleep but very aware that she was tossing and turning for hours, sweating and battling wave after wave of nightmares.

The moment she closed her eyes she began to dream that she was in that room with someone but it wasn't Peder who was in there with her. Where Peder had stood not two hours before, there was a woman at the window instead with her back to Anna, wearing a flowing white nightgown. She looked very spectral, very surreal. She moved into the dream as if driven by an unseen hand, a hand that pushed her towards the woman whose forehead was pressed against the window, her thin white hand resting on the glass by her cheek. Anna slowly approached the woman, not certain she wanted to see the woman's face, but as she lifted her head and looked right at Anna, she could see that it was her mother.

Chapter 10

The dream stayed with her well into the daylight hours, through her morning routine and into her quiet time at the library. She could still see her mother's face, the way you can still see the outline of an object bathed in sun when you close your eyes. Against her better judgment she decided to find Peder and tell him about her dream. She found him in the day room reading a battered copy of *Wuthering Heights*, his brow furrowed and a slight frown playing across his lips as his eyes moved over the words. Sitting down next to him, she gave him a moment to emerge from the world of Emily Bronte before speaking.

"How are you?" He asked, a deeper frown clouding his face as he took in the circles under her eyes and the pallor of her skin.

"I've been better," she said, sighing and folding her hands in her lap. She bent forward, signalling to him that she wanted to talk privately, and he leaned toward her until she could feel his breath on her neck. Their closeness set her nerves fluttering and she cleared her throat uncomfortably. "I was outside in the courtyard near the cafeteria when something caught my eye. The curtain in that window moved again and this time I saw a hand on the glass, right in the spot…"

"Right in the spot where there happens to be a slightly smudged handprint that we both saw?" Peder finished.

Anna nodded, swallowing hard. "It startled me so badly that I fell, but when I looked up again there was nothing there." Then she thought about what he had just said and something struck her. "What did you just say?"

"Hmm? Oh. I said something about the handprint."

"You said, the handprint we both saw. I thought you said you never remembered anything after these little sojourns of yours."

Peder looked caught, his cheeks and ears reddening under Anna's gaze. "Well, yes normally that's true but for some reason I remember that handprint. What else happened? You look as if you haven't slept." Peder quickly changed the subject, looking Anna over from disheveled head to toe.. "You're beginning to look like me," he added with a shaky chuckle.

"See that's the thing…" Frowning at his evasiveness, Anna began to tell him about her dream. When she had finished, Peder leaned back in his chair, his hands tented in front of his face in a thoughtful posture. "I don't want to frighten you but that's how it started for me, with the dreams."

Anna was silent for a moment, trying to find an answer that wouldn't come out sounding rude. "I appreciate your opinion but I don't think this is the same thing."

Peder shrugged off Anna's barb. "Maybe you're right. Maybe my thinking is skewed considering my experiences."

"Skewed," she scoffed. "I suppose so. All I know is that the dream was so powerful I woke up feeling as if it was real. I almost felt as if she was still here, still alive."

"I'm sorry, I didn't realize she had passed." Peder looked sympathetic. He tried to put his hand on Anna's knee but she moved away and resettled herself in her chair leaving him looking rather disappointed. Sitting back in his chair he went on, "Well, for now take the dream with a healthy dose of skepticism and try to figure out what your subconscious is telling you." He sighed, a deep regretful sound. "But I do suggest you keep all of this between us, for your own sake, because no one will understand, it will sound crazy to everyone else." He gestured to his institutional garb-- the gray pants and matching top that always made the men look as if they had just rolled out of bed.

She couldn't help thinking, rather unkindly, that he was trying to turn her dream into some kind of shared secret between them, but maybe he was right. For now she would keep the dream to herself; there was no need to go around blabbing about it. She stood abruptly, nearly knocking her chair so hard with the backs of her knees that it rocked a few times before settling back on all fours. "Thank you for listening. I should get back."

"I have all the time in the world to listen," Peder said, tucking his hands under his chin and turning to stare out the window at the sunlight that slanted down into the interior courtyard and bounced off the window panes of the hallway that led to the female wards.

That night when she closed her eyes and dropped off to sleep, she was immediately transported to that room once again and her mother was waiting for her. This time though, when Anna tried to take a step towards her mother, her feet wouldn't move; they felt like they were encased in lead. She tried to call out but couldn't make a sound. The spectre of her mother rocked its head back and forth, back and forth, making a sound like an animal in pain, a fisher cat crying out in the woods. The sound built, filling the room until Anna was afraid her head might burst. As the sound crescendoed and Anna felt she could no longer stand the noise, the figure turned around, its face twisted and its eyes hollow and gaping.

Anna woke, her mouth open in a silent scream, sweat pouring down her face and her hair plastered to her forehead. For days after she woke up the same way, feeling as if the night had passed in the space of minutes, the remains of the dream haunting her. She tried her best to hide the circles under her eyes; every morning she looked in the mirror after showering only to see that the hot water had done nothing for the black shadows that clouded her face. Of course it wasn't long before Harper noticed the change in her as the sleepless nights drained her, making her edgy and jumpy, prickly and moody.

"What's wrong with you Gilman? You're not your usual chipper self these days."

"I'm fine," Anna snapped. "I just have a lot on my plate."

Harper gave her a look that said she called bullshit, but she kept her tone light. "We should take a break. Relax, maybe have a picnic down by the lake or something." Harper looked sideways at Anna who was sitting dumbly at a table in the day room, staring off into space.. "What do you say? I won't take no for an answer Gilman."

She tried to ignore Harper's blatant staring. "Is that an order Dr. Westcott?" she deadpanned without cracking a smile.

"Yes it is." Harper said humorlessly. "Doctor's orders."

"Fine."

"Fine." Watching Harper's back as she stomped off the ward, Anna took a deep breath. She knew she shouldn't be taking her stress out on Harper but she didn't want to be needled and she didn't want to be bossed. Now she was stuck having a picnic with a psychiatrist.

That evening Harper knocked on Anna's door promptly at 6:00 to find her still in her work clothes. "Chop chop my dear. Fun waits for no man. Or woman as the case may be." She eyed Anna's wardrobe meaningfully and jerked her head towards the closet. "Think you might want to change?"

Anna looked down at herself as if she had forgotten what she was wearing. "Oh, I supposed I should, shouldn't I."

"Yes you should." Harper pointed at a hole in the thigh of Anna's jeans, a spot that had gotten snagged on the handle of one of the trash bins. "You may want to chuck that pair. Looks like they're a little worse for wear."

"They're fine," Anna shrugged, pulling them off and throwing them back into her closet. She traded her dirty tee shirt for a clean, yet still shapeless crew neck and pulled on a wrinkled pair of overalls. "Let's go."

Harper said nothing about Anna's choice of wardrobe and instead steered her friend out the door and down to the lake where she had stashed a large cooler. She grabbed a plaid blanket off of it and shook it out, laying it down on the grass. She had a bag slung over her shoulder that Anna hadn't even noticed and emptied the contents-- two plates, cups, silverware, and napkins- onto the blanket. They sat next to each other silently as Harper dished out fried chicken and mashed potatoes which Anna didn't touch in spite of how good it smelled. She knew if she dug in she would eat until she popped. She hadn't tasted food since breakfast the day before. Just the idea of eating made her stomach roll.

"Ok, spill it. What's wrong with you?"

Anna stared out across the lake and shrugged. "Nothing. I'm fine."

"You're so far from fine, you couldn't see fine if you looked over your shoulder." Harper turned sideways and grabbed Anna's hands, forcing her to look at Harper.. "Whatever is going on in that head of yours, you can tell me about it. It stays between us and I promise not to analyze you."

For the first time in days Anna chuckled. "You say that now, but you won't be able to resist."

Harper held up two fingers and put her right hand over her heart. "Scout's honor."

"Fine," she sighed. "I've been having nightmares, terrible ones where I wake up thinking they're real, that they really happened."

"Ok. Sounds normal so far. What else?"

"I've been seeing things."

Harper cocked her head and narrowed her eyes-- her "I'm listening" stance that Anna had seen her use with patients. "What kind of things?"

"Just one thing. A person. Well,so far just a hand to be specific." She told Harper about the room, the one she was also visiting in her dreams. She told her about the moving curtain, the handprint on the window.

Shaking her head, Harper grabbed a piece of chicken and bit into it. Anna listened to her chew, waiting for Harper to say she was crazy, or worse, laugh at her.

Harper filled their glasses with Coke, then began to carefully assure Anna that what she was seeing and dreaming was likely just a byproduct of stress. Harper reminded her that she had moved to an unfamiliar state, jumped into graduate school, then moved a *second* time to a hospital with a questionable future, all in short order. It was only natural that she should experience some stress reactions. "It manifests itself differently in everyone my dear. Not to mention all those residual feelings about your mother's death."

Anna looked up at her, shocked. "How did you know about my mother?"

Harper smirked. "Lucky guess." Anna didn't believe that for a minute. "Ok fine. Valerie told me. Listen, I wouldn't worry about it. The more you worry, the more stress you'll endure. The more stress, the more often the dreams will happen." She took a sip of her Coke and rested her cup on her knee. "Vicious circle."

Nodding, Anna saw the logic in what Harper was saying. She was stressed. There were constant changes at the hospital-- new patients, cuts in funding, the crumbling buildings. Then there was Peder, who made her monstrously uncomfortable yet each time she saw him her pulse quickened, her heart jumped, her breathing stopped. He talked in a way that was meant to be casual but most certainly did not *feel* casual. Anna realized she had drifted away and Harper was still talking.

"In the meantime, we need to find a way to get those nightmares under control so you can get some sleep." Harper drained her glass, refilled it, and topped off Anna's again. "Honestly, I think an anti anxiety might be a good quick fix for you."

"You really think so?" Anna had grown leery of medications after seeing so many friends get hooked on them until they no longer eased their symptoms. To her, medications were a slippery slope to electroshock and four point restraints.

Harper nodded. "I think so, yes. At the very least it'll give you the chance to get some sleep and maybe get rid of those circles under your eyes. You look like hell my friend."

"I'm aware. Though I have to say I've been avoiding the mirror lately."

Wiggling her eyebrows Harper said, "I can see why."

Anna smiled, giving in and popping a piece of chicken in her mouth. She chewed slowly and felt herself finally relax as Harper expertly changed the subject and began to ramble on about her rounds, the hospital's overall fate, and the future of psychiatric medicine in general.

"I don't know what I'm going to do when this place finally closes." Leaning back on her elbows, Anna closed her eyes and tilted her face to the sky.

"I think we've got a ways to go before that happens." Harper was convinced that they still had years to go before Westborough would be emptied completely. "Why else would they keep sending more patients?"

She made a good point. Anna had a hard time agreeing with the concept of deinstitutionalization. From everything she had read in the library she had learned that communities hadn't been ready to receive hundreds of mentally ill patients being released from the asylums. There was even a rumor that after Northampton State

Hospital had closed the police arrested more than one hundred patients trying to get back *in*. The asylum was the only life they had ever known and it was ripped away from them. "This place has become home."

"Agreed. Speaking of which, I've been thinking about moving out of the dorms."

"What do you mean?"

Apparently Harper had her eye on a room in one of the houses at the back of the campus. She had been offered a full time position on the medical staff and she could now have her pick of living quarters. She had her eye on the little gray cottage at the far end, closest to the corn fields. "It has a beautiful view and it's somewhat secluded from the rest of the campus. It only has two bedrooms so I'll only have one roommate at the most, which is nice. There's plenty of room for my furniture and I can finally make my coffee the way I like it. Not like that horrid sludge they serve in the kitchen."

Anna had never had a roommate, not even at college. She had fought for a single, using her only child status as an excuse to be alone, but Harper was fearless in new situations. "Wow, congratulations. That sounds pretty great."

Grinning, Harper held up her glass. "A toast. To setting up housekeeping. And new beginnings." Harper clinked her glass against Anna's and polished off the remainder of her soda.

"Here's to it."

Chapter 11

Christmas came just after Harper moved into the cottage. She took a break from unpacking to help decorate the tree in the day room. "I hate these nasty fake things they have on the wards," Harper complained, twisting a metal arm and watching as it flopped hopelessly at a right angle. "They look anemic with their bendy metal arms and half assed fake foliage." She shivered dramatically as she hung a red plastic ornament on a middle branch. They had strung the tree with white lights and were in the middle of hanging the mismatched collection of ornaments that had been kicking around in the hospital attic for decades.

"I wish they would get real ones for the patients. Just so they could enjoy the smell and something that actually looks like Christmas."

Harper closed her eyes and hugged an ornament to her chest. "The smell is the best part."

Anna laughed and hung a snowy white globe next to Harper's red one. "It most certainly is."

She and Harper had planned to spend Christmas Eve in the day room singing carols and watching *It's a Wonderful Life*. It was the only time of year the male and female patients were allowed to mix and there would be popcorn and hot cocoa. The ward staff had purchased small gifts for each of the patients that they would spend the evening wrapping in time to put under the tree after lights out.

Putting the finishing touches on the tree, Anna watched out of the corner of her eye as Peder came into the day room, dragging a chair into the far corner where he settled down to read. When the tree was finished and Harper had left to help wrap gifts, Anna headed for the closet to put away the ornament boxes. As she passed, Peder looked up and smiled.

"Merry Christmas Anna." She watched as he dug into the chair cushion and presented her with a small package that was carefully wrapped in scraps of newspaper. "This is for you. It's not much but I saw it and had one of the ward staff pick it up. I hope you like it."

Taking the package, Anna turned it over in her hands, trying to look pleased with the gift but she didn't actually appreciate such an intimate gesture, especially once she noticed the detail in the wrapping. It seemed that each strip of paper had been chosen with a purpose, each word had a meaning. Here the word heart. On the back, the word understanding. Dreams, depth, marvelous. Heat, passion, relief. Had she somehow given Peder the wrong impression by confiding in him?

"Peder," she said quietly. "I can't accept this." It was like a hidden message. To everyone else it would look like nothing more than yesterday's news. To Anna it looked more like a love letter, one that she didn't want. She handed the package back to him, her eyes fixed on the floor.

His face grew dark and he shifted in his seat. "Don't be so prudish Anna. It's just a book." He ripped it from her hands and tore off the wrapping, dropping the scraps on the floor. "It was being discarded from the hospital's library and I asked if I could have it. I was just being nice."

In a perfect world, Anna would have met Peder out in the real world somewhere, maybe at a book shop or a cafe. He would not have been sick, would not have been considered violent. They would have had coffee together or gone out to see a movie. Instead he was here, in a rage, making a scene over a book. The pure disgust in his eyes made Anna take a step back.

Peder stood and thrust the book back into her hands and storomed out of the day room, knocking into Harper's shoulder as he passed.

"What was that all about?" Harper asked as Anna bent to retrieve the crumbled paper from the floor.

Anna handed her the book and shook her head. "He tried to give me this. It was all wrapped in words, romantic words. And when I told him I couldn't accept it, he threw a tantrum."

Turning the book over in her hands, Harper frowned. "*The Great Gatsby,* eh? I hope it's not symbolic."

"What do you mean?" Anna asked, tossing the paper in the bin.

"Gatsby, he's in love with a woman he can't have." She handed it back to Anna, holding it with the tips of her fingers as if it was poison. "He kills himself in the end."

Anna sank down in the now empty chair and ran her fingers over the blue and yellow cover with its surreal floating eyes hung above a horizon of pouty red lips. Was Harper right that this was symbolic? If that was the case, did that mean Peder was in love with her? She had never thought of herself as attractive but somehow she must have something that appealed to him.

Leaning on the arm of the chair, Harper put a reassuring hand on Anna's shoulder. "I wouldn't worry about it. He's under close watch here. Just try to keep your distance if you can."

Harper left her sitting there, the book in her lap. It repulsed her, this gesture of whatever it was supposed to be. Love? Lust? Obsession? But just the same she was mesmerized by his gift and she wondered if this was how it was done, how people shared their feelings with members of the opposite sex. Anna had never been in a relationship, had never had a first date or a first kiss. Her mother was gone by the time Anna reached high school and she had been too devastated by the loss to even consider dating a boy. She never got the chance to talk to her mother about love, about romance.

Now her mother's face flashed before her, full of life with cheeks flushed and eyes bright, and Anna suddenly realized just how little she knew about either of her parents. Now that they were both gone she would never know how they met, if they courted, how he proposed. She remembered one of them saying they grew up in the same town but had they gone to school together? Had they had mutual friends, or did they meet by chance? By the time Anna was in junior high it seemed like her parents had very few friends. They didn't go to parties and rarely had people over for dinner that Anna could recall, yet they must have been happy at some point. Somewhere she remembered seeing a photograph of them at their wedding, smiles wide and bright, but that photograph had disappeared a long time ago.

Anna decided to take a walk before the festivities, clear her head a bit. Memories of her parents were dangerous, murky waters in which to tread. Her earlier memories of childhood were mixed. There had been trips to the Buffalo Zoo, visits to the New York State Museum. She had a postcard of one of the dinosaurs at the Buffalo Museum of Science and a cup from Niagara Falls. Sh even remembered holding her mother's hand as they crossed the border into Canada. But she also remembered the fights, the arguments that sometimes got so intense and last for so many days that her mother would send her away to her Aunt Sarah's house in Lackawanna. Sarah never asked questions; she knew Teresa and Malcolm were having problems.

Sarah also knew *why* they were having problems but she refused to tell Anna no matter how she begged. She said that it didn't concern her, that children shouldn't be involved in their parents' difficulties. "But I'm not a child," Anna would argue. Her aunt would always laugh at her niece's childish resolve, hug her, and send her outside to play.

Dropping Peder's book-- her book now she supposed- in her room, Anna wandered out to the courtyard and sat on the low stone wall. She touched the spot where she tripped though it felt exactly as concrete should-- cold and gritty. Of course, what had she expected? That it would be warm? Soft? "Of course not. It's just a curb." It was good that she could still laugh at her own silly notions, but still she couldn't help casting a glance at the window in the old ward. It was dark though, the winter sun casting a harsh reflection of the clouds in the glass. Anna had stupidly forgotten to put on a coat and she shivered in the waning light. That was the one thing she hated most about winter. She could tolerate the cold and the snow, but she hated the way the sun began to set mere hours after lunch and it was completely dark by the time dinner was ready to be served. The shortened daylight hours depressed her and made her want to stay inside until spring.

A cold breeze picked up and it lifted the collar on Anna's sweater, blowing her hair across her face and sending chills down her spine. She pulled her cardigan close across her chest and headed back inside. Taking one last look at the empty window, she pulled open the door, welcoming the rush of warm air, the lilt of cheerful voices floating down the stairwells and drawing her back to the ward.

The entire floor was gathered in the day room, men and women, patients and staff, all standing around the tree waiting for it to be lit. When Harper spotted Anna at the back of the crowd she shouted, "It's about time Gilman! We were all waiting for you!" Everyone chuckled, their eyes drifting back to the tree, and Harper began to lead a rousing countdown. "Five, four, three, two…" An orderly reached down and plugged in the tree while the patients cheered and began to sing.

After a few choruses of Jingle Bells and Silent Night, they started the film and Anna watched for a bit, the patients laughing and singing along with Jimmy Stewart. She looked around the room at the happy, placid faces until she spotted Peder, tucked into his corner once again. He caught her eye and frowned, then turned away, pretending to be interested in the movie. Her cheeks burned, and she felt anger rise in her throat. How dare he put her in this position and make her feel like she had done something wrong in trying to refuse his gift?

Getting up from her seat, Anna huffed out of the day room and stormed down the hall. Before she realized it she was turning the corner into the closed ward, taking the steps into the atrium that led to the peeling hallway. She reached the room at the end and was almost disappointed to find it empty, the window suddenly clean, the curtains where they belonged. Anna stood at the window and looked out over the courtyard where a light snow was beginning to fall-- it would be a white Christmas after all. She smiled to herself and turned to leave when a breath of cold air whipped through the room and made the curtains shiver. Like someone breathing on cold glass and drawing a message in the fog, a handprint slowly appeared on the glass.

"What do you want from me?" Anna whispered, but the moment she began to yell the window cleared and the handprint disappeared, the curtains falling still. She was losing her mind, she was sure of it. Maybe Harper was right and she did need to be medicated.

Chapter 12

After her mother's funeral Anna was sent to her aunt's house for what would turn out to be the last time. When her father pulled up to her aunt's house, he left her in the car while he and Sarah talked. Anna cracked the window just enough so she could hear her father beg her mother's sister to take her. He said it would only be a two week stay but as the end of the second week came and went, Anna knew she would not be going home. Her father had called one afternoon while she was out in the garden, but she had heard the phone ring and snuck in the back door to eavesdrop. Malcolm told Sarah that he couldn't take his daughter back, not after everything that had happened with Teresa. Her aunt had listened politely to while he told her he needed to leave Buffalo and he couldn't possibly take Anna with him.

"I'm putting the house up for sale Sarah."

She heard her aunt sigh as she switched the receiver to her other ear and reached into the sink to start the dishes. "She's your daughter Malcolm and she just lost her mother. What do you think it's going to do to her if she loses you too?"

Anna was crouched in the mud room just inside the door and she put her hand over her mouth to keep herself from crying out. Her father was leaving?

"I can't even look at her Sarah. How can I be a father to her?"

"You just do Malcolm. You just do." A dish clattered into the sink and Sarah swore, nearly losing her grip on the phone. "If you leave her now, she will never forgive you. And neither will I."

Of course Anna couldn't hear what her father was actually saying but she could imagine. Deep inside she had expected him to be cold, distant even, but she hadn't expected him to abandon her.

Sarah lowered her voice almost as if she knew Anna was there listening, and fired her final shot. "It's not what Teresa would want if she was here."

"Well she's not here now is she? And whose fault is that?"

"You have to be kidding me," Sarah hissed. "You can't possibly blame your daughter for what happened to my sister. If you do, then maybe you're right, you're not a father." With that she slammed down the phone and leaned over the sink to weep where her tears would mingle with the wash water. The water from the faucet muffled the sounds of her crying but Anna caught the sound of a sniffle here and there.

Anna remembered running from the mud room, out into the garden, to the far edge where there was a pond. She had stared into its placid surface, wondering what it would be like to climb into it, lay down in the water and let it cover her, rise over her face, her eyes, her nose until the air drained from her lungs and she went to sleep. By the time her aunt rushed out to the pond Anna was up to her knees in the water, ready to slip below the surface. Sarah plunged in after her and picked her up by her elbows, lifted her out of the pond, and pushed her down on the lawn.

"Anna Gilman, what do you think you're doing?"

Anna began to cry, balling her fists and pounding them against her soaking wet knees. "Daddy's leaving. He's going away and he's not taking me with him."

Sarah sunk down next to her and gathered Anna in her arms, ignoring the wet that seeped through her dress. "Oh honey. You were listening to me talk weren't you." Anna leaned into her aunt's shoulder and nodded miserably. "It's ok. You're here now and I'm never going to leave you. This is your home now."

Sarah had led Anna inside, stripped her of her wet clothes, and made her a cup of hot tea. Wrapped in a blanket, Anna tucked herself into the corner of her aunt's couch and stared out at the pond, wishing Sarah hadn't caught her, but grateful that she had. They never spoke of the incident again but sometimes Anna would catch her aunt watching her more carefully, her eyes following Anna around the house. Sometimes when she was outside, if she got too close to the pond, Sarah would knock on the kitchen window and shake her head.

Sometimes her father would call to check in, but never to speak directly to Anna. He also sent money, plenty of money, but never a birthday gift or Christmas card. Eventually the phone calls from her father dwindled until one day Anna realized he hadn't called in nearly three months. In fact they didn't hear from her father again until he sent a wedding announcement, which arrived two weeks after the actual wedding, and it was accompanied by a change of address card with a forwarding address in Florida, as if Anna would have written to him. Hardly. He had made his choice and now he had a new wife, likely a new family. Five years later he too passed away; Anna did not attend the funeral.

She always wondered if someday she would regret not having gone to her father's funeral but here she was, twenty five years old, still waiting for that moment to come, for that twinge of guilt, but it never did. Instead she felt the crushing shame of having let her mother go so easily, for not having tried harder to stay her little girl. She knew now that most mother daughter relationships were tense, that as a teenager she was meant to challenge her mother's authority and she was expected to reject her mother's friendship and counsel, but now that her mother had been dead for more than ten years, she felt the crushing weight of regret at the lost of their relationship. From that, she believed, she would never recover.

Now here she was, sitting in her room with her feet propped on the radiator, her journal propped on her knees. Tipping her chair back, she stared out over the lake, the light's reflection blinding her momentarily and leaving little trails of sunbursts behind her eyes. She rubbed them fiercely and realized her hands had come away wet and there were hot tears sliding down her cheeks. Swiping at them, Anna picked up her pen and continued writing down everything she could remember from that horrible time right after her mother's death. Valerie had been right, writing was cathartic. It also helped pass the time on days when she couldn't find anything to keep her busy; she had to keep moving or else she would stop and think in circles until she wanted to scream.

Closing her journal, Anna pulled on a pair of boots and her coat. It was a good day for a walk, the snow having been cleared, the chill in the air having disappeared for a little while. Her hair was hanging loose down her back, her cheeks pink with windburn from being out on a few of the coldest days of the season. She wound her way through the ward and took the stairway down to the first floor, passing Valerie's empty office and out the front door. She hung a left towards the Talbot Building that used to be part of the Lyman School for Boys, a reform school that had moved to its new home farther down Route 9 in 1847. Anna loved the curved red brick of the bay windows on the largest building, her favorite. She imagined the building would be cozy inside with fireplaces in some of the rooms and overstuffed antique furniture.

Behind Talbot was Codman, another brick mansion, and behind that the auditorium and the laundry, the path winding back around the main building to the docks where Anna emptied the trash every night. Shipping and receiving connected directly to the cafeteria with its grand double green doors that reached from the stoop to the roof line. Across from the cafeteria was a driveway that led down behind a building that was only connected to the main hospital by tunnels. Walking down the drive Anna slipped through the fence onto the cracked basketball courts behind the Robert F. Kennedy School. She knew there were kids inside that building, kids who had been convicted of various crimes and were serving their time in a Department of Youth Services building that overlooked the old wards. Anna wondered what they imagined when they looked out at the monstrous asylum.

There were walking trails that circled the campus but Anna stuck to the paved road that brought her into another courtyard where the staff from some of the other wards took their breaks. The courtyard was bisected by an above ground walkway that dead ended in stairs that went right back up to the old wards. There was a covered porch that jutting out into the courtyard as well and, ducking between the stone columns, Anna headed back into the hospital and took the stairs to the second floor.

She knew she was on the opposite side of the wall from the window, separated by nothing more than a narrow passageway. This hallway was an odd shape because of the staircase and there were only four patient rooms and a restroom. The floorboards were beginning to warp from moisture that was slowly seeping in through the holes in the roof that were growing and spreading like a disease, leaving the wards exposed to the elements. There were naked bed frames pushed against the walls in each room, naked bulbs suspended from the plaster, covered in dust. Walking to the window Anna looked down the hill to the lake, the same view she had from her own room. Peeking inside the closets she could see there were still wooden hangers on the rods, metal hangers littered the floor.

Slipping through the passageway, Anna stood in the other hallway, marveling at the way the sunlight spilled from the open rooms and criss-crossed the hallway floor. For the first time since she came to Westborough she took the time to look in the other rooms on that floor. The first door was larger than the others, painted hunter green. The name of the room's occupant was long gone and when Anna tried to open the door it stuck, making a loud sucking noise as she thrust her weight against it. The wood was swollen, the paint peeling off in sheets taking with it splinters that stuck out like javelins as it started to open under a great deal of protest. Anna gave the bottom of the door a swift kick and pushed it open though it ground to a halt on the rotted floor inside, leaving just barely enough room for her to slip through.

Here the roof had caved in completely, shingles and tarpaper laying in a soggy heap in the corner. The floor was coated in slick green moss, the walls blooming with green and black spiders of mold that flowered in the cracks that spanned the walls. The only thing left in the room was a rotting wood cabinet that hung precariously off one wall, its doors sagging open and reaching for the floor. At some point there would be nothing left of this room and nature would reclaim it completely.

Pulling the door shut behind her, Anna wandered across the hall into a sunny patient room that had light pink walls and a peeling linoleum floor. From the window she could see the covered walkway and the two courtyards on either side, one with its designated smoking area, the other with picnic tables and a wooden bench swing for the staff. If you ignored the purpose of the building and its grounds, it was a very beautiful place.

Here in the light of day Anna suddenly felt silly for thinking of this entire hallway as anything more than an empty space. Wandering through the remaining rooms, she marveled at the shadows the trees cast on the bare floors, the way the light moved when it was uninhibited by furniture and blinds. Finally she crossed the threshold into the last room on the right. Sunlight shot through the windowpane and bent at odd angles, up the walls that looked far more cream than gray.

"It's just a room," she whispered aloud. Walking over to the window, Anna leaned against the window frame, her hands on the sill, and watched the birds pick through the snow outside the cafeteria, hoping for crumbs.

"It's not just a room and you know it."

Peder's voice behind her made her jump. "My God Peder. You can't sneak up on someone like that."

"I'm sorry. I saw you roaming around and figured you'd come up here."

Anna folded her arms across her chest and scowled. "Of course you did," she snapped. "And it is just a room. Look around you. There's nothing here Peder!"

He bared his teeth in a wolfish smile. "Yes there is. There's something here and now it's crept into your dreams Anna." He took a step toward her, leaning forward into the empty space between them. "That's why you're here in the middle of the day trying to convince yourself that it's just an empty room."

"It is just a room," she growled, then pushed past him. He did not reach out to stop her, nor did he call after her. Turning the corner into the atrium, she glanced over her shoulder but Peder was no longer in the hallway. He had gone inside the room.

Chapter 13

That night, when she tucked herself into bed, she tried her best to calm her nerves, put Peder and his nonsense out of her head, but no matter how she tried, she kept thinking maybe he was right about that room. Grabbing the library book about the Fox sisters, Anna settled in to read and tried to relax in spite of the persistent early darkness of winter. She thought maybe she could purge herself of some of the fear and anxiety that room had instilled in her, perhaps she would be able to sleep soundly for once.

She fell asleep, the book still in her hands, to find herself in that dream yet again, in that room standing before the same specter with its back to her. It was knocking on the windowpane, and even in her dream Anna realized that her readings about the Fox sisters were carrying over into her dreams, but suddenly the knocking turned to whispers and the voice was her mother's.

"The sidewalk," it muttered. The spirit looked down, out the window to the courtyard, still knocking on the glass. "The sidewalk," it repeated quietly. When it looked back at her, it was her mother's face again, her eyes bright and her skin supple, a healthy flush in her cheeks. She looked exactly as she did the last time Anna saw her.

"Mother!" Anna cried, trying to rush forward but something held her back, some unseen hand that would not allow her to go to her mother.

Instead the thing that looked like her mother smiled. "There were roses, Anna. There were roses."

Tears welled in Anna's eyes at the sight of her mother's smile. "Roses where mom? At Aunt Sarah's?" Her aunt had been famous in Lackawanna for her prize winning rose garden and it had been her favorite place to sit and read when she was younger.

Her mother shook her head sadly and Anna watched in dismay as the shape of her body began to fade away. "No dear, on the sidewalk. There were roses all along the sidewalk, and I thought of you." As her mother's image turned to smoke, Anna felt a warmth creep through her, but with it was a feeling of sadness and confusion. What did her mother mean, the sidewalk? What sidewalk? What roses?

Anna woke the next morning feeling as if she had forgotten something important, or lost something she needed, but then she remembered her dream, remembered speaking with her mother. She got out of bed and picked through her closet, looking for something a little bit nicer to wear, finding a pair of jeans that was neither wrinkled nor ripped, and a pale pink sweater that she pulled on over a collared shirt. Standing in front of the mirror, Anna looked at herself, really looked, for the first time in ages and she saw someone she barely recognized. Her hair was a mess, her face pale and drawn. "I think it's time to do something about that," she said, rummaging in the top drawer of her dresser for what was left of her cosmetics.

Climbing the stairs, Anna ran her hands through her freshly brushed hair and smoothed her sweater. As she rounded the corner to the nurses' station, still in a fog of satisfaction at her makeover, Anna ran smack into Harper who was preparing for rounds. "Good lord Harper I'm so sorry. I didn't even see you there!" Anna put her hand to her chest to steady her racing heart.

Harper was looking at her funny, taking in Anna's reasonably well-coiffed hair and crimson cheeks. "Since when do you wear lipstick?"

Anna raised her fingers guiltily to her lips that were smeared with an iridescent gloss. "Well actually, just this morning. I took our conversation down by the lake to heart-- you know, when you said I looked terrible- and decided to do something about it."

Eyebrows shooting up, Harper chuckled. "Fair point. Though as your friend, I can tell you the shiny lips and mascara still aren't doing much for the bags under your eyes that are now halfway to your chin."

"I know. But it's a start." Forcing a laugh, Anna ran her hands through her hair and smoothed down her sweater.

"Are you sleeping?"

She nodded, looking down at her hands, the nails bitten and torn. "I am, but I'm still having the same dream." Harper sighed, then reached into her pocket for her prescription pad.

"Here." Harper scribbled something illegible on the top slip and handed it to Anna. "Take this to the dispensary and they'll fill it for you. It's for anxiety but it'll help you sleep. Only take it at night and only when you know you can get a full night's sleep, otherwise you'll be more of a zombie than you already are."

Anna nodded, stuffing the piece of paper in her pocket as she headed to the day room to clean up. Her plan was to wipe down all the chairs and tables before the next group session, but now she was distracted by the piece of paper burning a hole in her pocket.

Maybe it really was time for her to do something about her nightmares, about the sleeplessness that no doubt would take over eventually. She thought back to some of those nights as a teenager at her Aunt Sarah's when she would lay awake until the early hours of the morning, unable to fall asleep. Once her aunt realized what was happening she gave Anna a healthy dose of cough medicine that knocked her right into a dreamless, weightless sleep.

"In the morning," she whispered to herself. "I'll fill it in the morning."

She got to work straightening the day room and was elbow deep in disinfectant when the wall phone rang. She looked to see if there was anyone around to answer but everyone else seemed otherwise engaged so Anna answered it instead. "C Ward. How may I help you?"

"Ah yes. This is Dr. Brown in clinical." Brown cleared his throat again and Anna could hear papers being shuffled. "Is Miss Martin available? I need to speak with her immediately. It seems there have been reports of some patient wanderings into the closed wards."

Anna was surprised. She had assumed Peder's sojourns to the back wards would be logged but she hadn't expected the incidents to make it all the way to the head of clinical's desk. "She's not available at the moment but I can certainly let her know you called."

"Tell her this needs to be handled yesterday." The receiver clicked in her ear and she heard the dial tone. Dr. Brown had just hung up on her! This was just what Valerie needed, Brown breathing down her neck about a patient. From what she had heard from Harper he was a bear to deal, a miserable old windbag whose retirement was long overdue. Anna thanked her lucky stars she didn't have to deal with him.

Another hour passed on the ward before a supervisor even checked in and it wasn't Valerie; Anna had forgotten it was her day off and Celeste, that bobble-headed gnome who couldn't even keep track of her own head, was filling in. Anna stopped her just outside the nurses' station and tried to get her attention.

"Celeste..." She ducked down so that she was in Celeste's direct line of sight. "Celeste, can you get a message to Valerie?"

"What is it dear?" Celeste finally focused and put her hand on Anna's arm as she spoke.

"Dr. Brown called. He wanted..."

"You took a call from Dr. Brown?" she interrupted, yanking her hand off Anna's arm as if she had been burned, her mouth widening in a perfect "O" of surprise.

"Yes, I...there was no one here so I picked it up."

Celeste clucked and shook her finger at her like you would at a naughty child. "Next time leave the phone to me. Did he know it was you?"

Anna shook her head. She honestly didn't think Dr. Brown knew anyone's name but Valerie's.

"Good. Good, thank goodness. What did he want?"

"He heard that there was a patient who kept wandering into the back wards. He didn't seem to know much about it but he wanted Valerie to handle it."

"Oh sugar." Celeste never swore and it infuriated everyone on the ward. If ever there was a time to say the actual word this was it. "I'll go take care of it. Now shoo."

"Yes ma'am." When Celeste's back was turned, Anna threw her a mock salute and stuck out her tongue.

"I saw that." Harper was standing in the doorway of the supply closet with boxes of file folders balanced in her arms. "Did I hear you say Brown called?"

With an exaggerated eye roll, Anna mimed slitting her throat. "Yes. He found out that Peder has been wandering around the old ward. Well, he didn't seem to know Peder's name but he's been made aware of it."

"Shit." Harper stamped her foot. "I knew this was going to happen. We caught him at it twice more this week alone. An orderly had to track him down and practically drag him back to his room."

Anna was surprised to hear that. No one had told her. "I didn't realize he was still doing it."

Harper nodded and looked down at her shoes. "I didn't want you to know. I didn't want you getting involved."

"No, I understand. I appreciate it."

"I know he gives you the creeps."

That wasn't too far off the mark. "What do you think will happen now that Brown knows?"

Harper shrugged. "Probably just a stern talking to about liability and a lecture on how not to embarrass him."

"You don't think anyone will get in trouble do you?"

"No." She shook her head and laughed. "He can't afford to discipline any of us directly. If one of us was to leave he'd have a hell of a time replacing us. It's not like there are qualified candidates just waiting in the wings to replace us."

Laughing Anna tossed her hair and realized, all jokes aside, that Harper was right. Even if Brown somehow found out that Anna had been in that room with Peder, what could he possibly do? "Then again," she laughed again. "All you really need to work here is a pulse and the ability to remain upright for a few hours at a time."

"True, but it's not like we even have any of those knocking down our door either!" Hefting her boxes of file folders, Harper turned to grab two packs of printer paper, a box of paper clips, and a pile of pens then kicked the door shut behind her. "I'm sure it'll be fine. I'll call him back myself and tell him we've got it handled. Then I'll ask him something about a case I'm working on and he'll talk for hours. He'll forget all about Peder."

Anna took the three packs of printer paper and followed Harper to the elevator. "Can I ask you a question about Peder?"

"Depends what the question is," Harper replied, eyeing her sideways.

"When he first got here you said he had been on the violent ward at Medfield. Can you tell me why?"

Harper sighed and looked away. "I can't. All I can tell you is that his stay there was court ordered."

Court ordered meant he had been sentenced to his time at Medfield by a judge. "So does that mean he committed a crime?"

"Looks like it." Harper nodded. "I honestly can't tell you more. Parts of his file are confidential even to me. My guess is there was some sort of assault and when they realized he was schizophrenic, he landed in emergency psych."

"Must have been one hell of an assault to land him in the violent ward."

The elevator doors slid open on the first floor and Harper stepped off, heading for her office that was around the corner from nursing supervisors. As she passed Valerie's door, Anna realized she hadn't talked with her in nearly two weeks and made a mental note to check in with her.

Dumping her supplies on top of her desk, Harper flopped

down in her leather desk chair and leaned back, closing her eyes. "This place gives me a migraine. And calling Brown back is only going to make it worse."

"You could always let Valerie handle it."

Harper shook her head. "No, it's fine. I don't mind doing it. I know just what to say to get him off topic. Valerie is too professional, she would end up getting caught in his miserable blathering about patient safety and whatnot."

"I suppose you're right. Well I'm going to go see if I can catch Valerie and check in with her." Heading down the hallway, Anna noticed that maintenance had taken to leaving the lights off during daylight hours, no matter how dark the day was outside, and the hallway outside of Valerie's office was particularly dark. There were no windows in her little corner of the rat maze so the only light came from the overhead fluorescents. When she poked her head in Valerie's office, she found her squinting under the light of a small desk lamp.

"Why is it so dark in here?"

Valerie looked up and smiled ruefully at Anna. "They've decided to save money by keeping the lights off during the day. That includes the one in my office since it's on the same switch as the hallway."

"You're kidding me. That's ridiculous." The lamp on her desk cast a paltry glow that barely lit up half the surface of your desk.

"I wish I was Anna." Taking off her glasses, Valerie sat back and rubbed her eyes. "What can I do for you?"

Anna shrugged. "Nothing in particular. I just realized I hadn't checked in for a while. I wanted to thank you again for that journal you gave me."

"Oh, you're very welcome." Valerie smiled and reached up to massage the muscles in her neck. "Are you finding it helpful?"

"Very much so." Tucking herself into the yellow plastic chair across from Valerie, Anna told her what she had been writing in her journal. Not specifics of course, but broad strokes. Enough to make Valerie smile even broader with apparent satisfaction. "Writing in it every day has certainly helped relieve some stress and help me settle in here."

Valerie nodded, then frowned. "Just remember what I said about settling in here."

"I know. I get it." With that Anna stood and ran her hands through her hair, nodding at Valerie. "Thanks for the advice."

"You're very welcome." Valerie watched as Anna turned to go. "Oh and Anna," she said as Anna glanced over her shoulder. "You're looking good these days. Relaxation works for you."

Anna laughed out loud and wiggled her fingers in a little wave. "Thanks Valerie. Have a good one."

That night, as she slept, Dr. Brown's voice invaded her dreams and reminded her that Peder needed to be handled. Tangled in her sheets, she dreamed of Peder but every time he spoke she heard Brown, muttering about patient wanderings. Then suddenly Peder's face was replaced by Brown's as he railed at her for snooping in the old wards, threatening to expel her from the hospital and fire Harper. She woke with a start, staring into the pitch black of her room, sweat rolling off her forehead and down her cheeks. As she stared up at the ceiling, she resolved to make the dispensary her first stop in the morning.

Chapter 14

Standing in line at the dispensary, Anna crumpled and smoothed the prescription in her hands over and over, a nervous habit. When it was her turn, she handed the sweaty wrinkled mess to the nurse and smiled sheepishly. "Sorry. I've been holding onto it for a while."

She didn't laugh, didn't even crack a smile as she turned to scan the shelves stacked with bottles. "Wait over there." She disappeared into the back and Anna sat down in the makeshift waiting room that overflowed into the ward's solarium. Picking up a tattered old copy of Better Homes and Gardens, Anna settled in on the salmon colored couch that had been pushed under a window in the solarium. As she flipped the dog-eared pages, she saw Peder out of the corner of her eye, joining the line at the dispensary counter. He had a book in his hand, an orderly at his elbow holding a stack of prescription slips, at least five of them. Anna tried not to stare but she couldn't imagine what it was like to have to take that many medications just to maintain control over yourself.

She watched as Peder shifted from foot to foot, frowning as the patient in front of him took her time unfolding a week old lunch menu as the nurse behind the counter explained to her that this wasn't the cafeteria. Just as she finally convinced the woman she was in the wrong place, another nurse appeared at the counter and called her name. "Anna Gilman. Come to the window please."

Peder turned slowly to watch as she approached the counter, but she kept her eyes on the ground, refusing to make eye contact with him. She flashed the nurse a tight smile as Anna took the medication from her, watching her head for the back to join the other nurse doing whatever it was they were doing back there. Threading her way to the other side of the line to avoid Peder, Anna yelped as Peder lunged forward and snatched the pills from her before she could react.

"Ativan," he crowed, letting out a low whistle. "Well, well. I see someone is having an issue with her anxiety," he hissed, venom in his voice.

"Give that to me. That's none of your business." Anna tried to keep her voice level; there was no sign of the orderlies who would surely rush them at the first sign of trouble so Anna tried not to push Peder's buttons.

"What's the matter Anna," he spat. "Having trouble with your conscience?"

Anna tried to grab the pills back from him but he held his hand high above her head where she wouldn't be able to reach it without jumping. "Stop it Peder. You don't know what you're talking about."

"I think I do. How are those nightmares of yours? Still having a hard time sleeping?"

"I told you that in confidence," she replied angrily.

"Well you obviously told someone else about it otherwise you wouldn't be taking medication." He leered at her. "Let's see who did you tell? Let me guess, Dr. Harper Westcott. Yes, that uppity bitch I always see you talking to."

Anna stopped reaching for the pills and her mouth fell open. "Don't call her that!"

"Did you tell her everything you told me? Hmm?" They were now standing next to an elderly gentleman who was talking to his hands, the line now snaking out the door and into the television room that was attached to the solarium.

"What business is it of yours if I did?"

"Because that was between us!" he roared, heads turning to stare at the ruckus they were causing. "That was our secret. I told you to keep it between us. I told you she would think you were crazy."

"Shut up!" Anna shouted back. Moving closer to Peder she lowered her voice and jabbed a finger into his chest, all pretense of keeping him calm completely shattered. "It's none of your business. And just because I confided in you doesn't mean there's anything between us. You were just someone to talk to."

His face darkened as if someone had switched off the light in his eyes. "There is something between us and you know it. That room brought us together, something in there ties us to one another."

Anna dug her fingernails into the back of Peder's hand and wrenched the pills away from him. Keeping her head down, she walked quickly out of the solarium, her eyes straight ahead.

She heard Peder's footsteps follow her into the hallway and stop just inside the solarium's double doors. "I know exactly who you are Anna Gilman!" he shouted after her. "I know all about you!"

As soon as she was out of sight of the solarium Anna started running and she didn't stop until she was safely in her room with the door closed. Just to be on the safe side, she took the chair from her desk and wedged it under her doorknob. Sitting on her bed, Anna dropped her head in her hands and tried to steady her breathing and slow her heart, trying to block out the sound of Peder's voice as he yelled down the hallway at her.

Of course there was the tiniest grain of truth to what he had said; Anna had confided in him because she had felt something of a connection, but he was wrong about it being anything more than kindred spirits. He had taken her confidences and blown it out of proportion, turning it into some sort of private conspiracy between the two of them. Anna pulled the chair away from her door and wrenched the knob, rushing out into the hall to the water fountain where she let it run until it was like ice. Filling a paper cup, she rushed back to her room, slammed the door, and replaced the chair under the knob.

She shook the bottle out of the bag and popped off the cap, pouring every last pill into the palm of her hand, the little white pills tumbling into a tiny pyramid. Much like that day at her aunt's pond, Anna wondered what it would feel like to swallow the entire pile at once, to feel that wave of nothingness wash over her and wipe out every last bad memory and every last bit of sadness and fear. She stared at them in her hand for what seemed like hours but was merely minutes before using the bottle to scoop all but one back in. Putting the cap back on, she stowed the pills in her top drawer, underneath her journal, and washed the pill down with a slug of water. So many things had changed since the incident at the pond and Anna knew that she didn't actually want to die, she wanted to be able to turn off her mind for a while. That miniature white oval would do just that as it disintegrated and coursed through her veins, like pressing the mute button on her thoughts.

Laying back, Anna stared up at the ceiling and began to count the cracks, waiting for the Ativan to kick in. Ten minutes passed but she felt nothing. The weightlessness she craved did not come, nor did the darkness in her mind. Sighing, she rolled onto her side and tried to close her eyes but each time she did she saw Peder's face, contorted with rage, yelling about knowing who she was. What did that mean, he knew who she was? Of course he knew who she was. They saw each other nearly every day.

As the minutes ticked by, Anna suddenly began to feel herself drifting away, her eyelids growing heavy, her limbs melting into themselves. Eyes closed, she fell into a deep and dreamless sleep for the first time in weeks. When she woke again night had fallen and her stomach was growling, but she was reluctant to head to the cafeteria on her own; though she wondered if Peder was crazy enough to start anything in the middle of the dinner rush.

Pulling on a sweater, Anna headed for the cafeteria where the smell of roasting chicken made her stomach rumble even harder. She stood on her tiptoes and scanned the crowd, searching for Peder and finding Harper instead. Relief washed over her and she dove into the throng of patients, pushing her way to her friend. "Harper, you won't believe what happened…"

But Harper was already frowning, her forehead creased with worry. "I'm betting I will because I've already heard about it from at least three patients and two orderlies, not to mention the phone call I got from the pharmacist at the dispensary."

Anna hung her head, embarrassment creeping into her cheeks. "I'm so sorry Harper."

"What do you have to be sorry for?" she barked. "From what everyone said Peder Roderick was harassing you and making a scene."

"A scene. Well, that's the understatement of the year. He grabbed my prescription and wouldn't give it to me, then started yelling about how I shouldn't have told you about my nightmares because now you were going to think I was crazy and how that was our secret."

Harper was shaking with anger, her fists clenched at her side like she was fighting the urge to find Peder and punch him, hard. "How did he know about your nightmares?"

"I told him," Anna admitted sheepishly. "You remember how I went to find him in the old wards a couple of times?" Harper nodded. "Well I felt bad for him after that because he had no idea why he kept going there and couldn't remember a thing. I told him about my dreams to make him feel better, let him know I understood what he was feeling."

"That wasn't the best idea you've ever had," Harper sighed. "But what's done is done. Now he thinks the two of you have some sort of private connection because you told him something he considered a secret. I'll have to let Dr. Brown know so that clinical can address it before it goes any farther."

"Do you think he would...you know…" Anna trailed off, afraid to ask what she was thinking.

"Hurt you? I suppose he could try but once I notify clinical he won't be allowed to go very far without supervision."

"They'll take away his privileges?"

Nodding, Harper grabbed a tray and reached for a salad, then added a brownie. "What?" she barked when she saw Anna eyeing her dessert choice. "I'm stressed. I need chocolate." She broke into a grin. "I'm an uppity bitch remember?"

Anna couldn't help but laugh at that. "I guess good news travels fast."

"Trust me, that was the first thing that got repeated. Not that Peder got in your face and nearly knocked you on your ass, but that he called me an uppity bitch." She shook her head and laughed with Anna. "I think George at the pharmacy took a special amount of pleasure in repeating that little tidbit."

Trailing after Harper, Anna grabbed a plate piled high with roast beef and mashed potatoes. They grabbed a seat in the corner of the cafe, closest to the heaters, and dug into their dinner.

"What else is bothering you?" Harper asked without even looking up from her plate.

"How do you know something is bothering me?"

Looking up, Harper pointed her fork at Anna's eyes. "I can just tell."

Sighing, Anna told her what Peder had said to her as she ran away like a scared little rabbit. "He said he knows all about me. What do you think that means?"

"I think," Harper said, her brownie halfway to her mouth, "that he's convinced himself that he knows something about you no one else does. I'm sure it all goes back to him thinking your nightmares were a secret between you two."

"I don't know. It seemed like something completely different to me, like he really does know something he shouldn't."

"Like what?"

Anna shrugged. "That's the problem. I have no idea."

"Have you started taking the medication yet?"

Anna nodded. "I did. Thank you."

"Make sure you take it regularly. It has to build up in your system in order to work."

"I know. I read the label. But let me tell you, I didn't have to wait for it. Those little pills sure pack a big punch"

Harper looked at her sideways and laughed. "Hit you like a ton of bricks?"

"Sure did. I slept soundly for almost five hours today."

"I bet that felt good."

"It felt amazing." It was such a relief to sleep without seeing her mother's face or hearing her voice. Harper was happy the medication had knocked her out so completely but she warned Anna that the effect wouldn't always be that absolute. Eventually, once the medication levels in her body had become stable, she would simply feel like the edges had been smoothed out. "I'm fine with that as long as I can finally get some sleep and start to feel human again."

"You might want to work on looking human too."

Anna looked up to find that Harper was joking and she took a forkful of mashed potatoes, flinging them right on the shoulder of Harper's lab coat. "Don't be mean!"

Laughing, Harper returned fire with a frisbee of cucumber that bounced off of Anna's cheek. They dissolved into giggles as Harper fingered the potatoes off her jacket and popped them in her mouth. "Ok, ok. I surrender. Let's call it quits before we start a full scale food fight."

Looking at Harper, Anna felt beyond grateful that she had found such a solid friend who understood her so well. As an only child Anna had always had difficulty making friends; she kept to herself through high school, then completely retreated from the rest of the world when her mother passed. The only person she ever considered a friend was her aunt which she knew didn't really count because she was family. For the first time in her life that she could honestly say she had a best friend, someone she could share everything with without the fear of being judged or ridiculed. Even though Harper's first duty was as a psychiatrist, she never made Anna feel as if she was a patient. She simply listened and offered suggestions the way any other friend would and for that Anna was profoundly grateful.

Harper stood and started collecting her dishes. "I'm going to go make some coffee in the break room. You want some tea?"

"That would be heaven. Let's go!" Anna dumped her own tray and followed Harper out the door to the back stairs. Together they loaded the coffee maker and put on a pot of water to boil for tea. While they waited, Harper told Anna about the first time she had to dissect a cadaver in medical school, how nervous she had been that she would throw up in front of everyone.

"I could literally feel myself turning green," she chuckled as she filled her mug with steaming hot coffee that was the consistency of molten asphalt.

"How can you drink that stuff?" Anna shivered, repulsed at the thought of Harper not just drinking it, but drinking it black, as she poured herself a cup of tea.

Shrugging, Harper took a healthy swig and swallowed hard. "You get used to it. I didn't used to be a coffee drinker but long nights and even longer rotations in medical school definitely required quite a bit of caffeine."

"I can only imagine." Her aunt was the one to introduce her to tea. Malcolm was a die hard coffee drinker like Harper but Teresa had preferred water, loathing the idea of pumping a stimulant through her veins, even one as benign as caffeine. On her first morning at Sarah's, Anna woke to the smell of something delicious cooking in the kitchen and when she wandered downstairs wiping the sleep from her eyes, her aunt presented her with a breakfast buffet the likes of which she had only seen on television. There was bacon, sausage, eggs, two kinds of toast, English muffins with their nooks and crannies swimming with butter, and a selection of herbal teas.

"The white teas are my favorite." Sarah already had a delicate flowered cup in her hand filled to the brim with a sweet smelling liquid that reminded Anna of the raspberry bushes in the neighbor's garden back home in Buffalo.

Taking the wooden tea box in her hands, Anna slowly picked up each flavor and sniffed it, trying to imagine what each different scent might taste like once it had been steeped in hot water. She settled on an Earl Grey with a pungent, mystical odor that made her think of Misselthwaite Manor in *The Secret Garden*. It smelled very British but with a hint of the Middle East, mysterious almost.

When she thought about that day, she could remember that first sip as if it had been that very morning. The moment the hot liquid touched her tongue she fell in love and became a ritual tea drinker. Every morning Sarah got up before her, and though the lavish breakfasts were relegated to Sundays only, tea was a daily staple. In the afternoon, when Anna got home from school, her aunt would have a snack waiting for her and dinner preparations underway. While she did her homework at the kitchen table, Sarah would chop, slice, and dice, humming to herself as she worked. After dinner they would settle in on the couch, Anna with a book, Sarah with her sewing, and they would let the TV play softly in the background while they waited for the water to boil. Since it was so close to bedtime, Anna's second cup of tea was always decaffeinated, usually a green tea of some kind.

As she stood with Harper and breathed in the scent of her English breakfast, a smile tugged at her lips as she pictured her aunt sipping from her good china. "I definitely prefer tea."

"Was your mother a tea drinker?"

Her heart leapt at the mention of her mother and she felt a lump rise in her throat as she shook her head. "No. My aunt was, her sister."

"Oh. I'm sorry. I didn't mean to upset you."

She shook her head and smiled sadly. "It's ok. You didn't upset me. Your question just caught me by surprise."

"You never talk about her. Your mother I mean."

"I know. It's been years but it's still so hard."

"How did she die?"

Shrugging, Anna's face fell. "I don't know to be honest." She could tell Harper wanted to press her for more but something in her expression must have stopped her.

"I'm so sorry Anna. I can't even imagine losing your mother like that."

"Thanks, but it was a long time ago." Ten years ago to be exact. Ten years, three months, and twelve days. Not that she was counting. "I should get going. That nap was good but I still have a lot of sleep to catch up on."

Putting her cup in the sink, she reached over and gave Harper a quick hug, then headed back to her room where she took another pill, then sank into darkness.

Chapter 15

The night her mother died they were in Niagara Falls for the weekend. She remembered her father hadn't wanted to go but her mother had insisted that they go because Anna was a teenager now and there would come a time when she would have better things to do than go on vacation with her parents. Malcolm had agreed, rather reluctantly, but the moment they crossed the border he seemed to loosen up a bit. The first thing they did was get dinner, though Anna could no longer picture the restaurant no matter how she tried. Holding her mother's hand they ducked in and out of tacky souvenir shops, laughing at the other tourists snapping up picture keychains and "I <3 NY" coffee mugs.

Anna also remembered the greatest reason for her father's reluctance to go to Canada. The last time they went away as a family Anna had been moody and difficult. Her mother laughed it off, saying it was natural, all teenage girls went through hormonal stages, but Malcolm had gotten angry, so angry that he refused to leave the hotel. Anna had locked herself in the bathroom and railed at them about how they had ruined her life and she was tired of being trapped in an existence that revolved around her parents. When she had finally allowed her mother to come into the bathroom, Teresa had found her in the bathtub, fully clothed, with the water from the overhead spray mingling with the tears that ran down her face.

This weekend Anna vowed would be different, better. No matter what happened she was going to behave herself. When they got home after the last time her parents had fought for days. Malcolm insisted that Anna's behavior was out of control. He berated Teresa for spoiling her daughter and allowing her to run wild. Teresa fought back, calling Malcolm an unfeeling tyrant, accusing him of refusing to understand his daughter's needs. She remembered her father saying, "What about what we need Teresa? It's been fifteen years of putting her needs first and look at the thanks we get." Anna hated when her parents fought, especially when she was the cause of it, as she so often was. She tried her hardest to do everything right but somehow she always managed to step out of line just enough to infuriate her father and ruin whatever occasion they were attempting to enjoy as a family.

Then her mother died. Anna didn't know what happened, only that she wasn't there, and by the time she got back to the hotel, her father was surrounded by Canadian police officers, a grim look on his face and his lips set in a tight line. He didn't say a word to her that night, or any night after for that matter. Her mother was gone and soon she would be shipped off to her aunt's.

Now, here she was in a strange bed, in a strange city, dreaming about the last night she had with her mother, the last time they were happy together. She tried to remember what their last conversation was, or even what she was wearing that night but it was those small details that eluded her memory. There was a time when just thinking of her mother conjured the scent of her perfume or the sound of her laugh, but now when she thought of her mother, all she could picture was the woman who smiled back at her from photographs. The woman who no longer aged, who existed only in those stolen moments on film that were now collecting dust in her Aunt Sarah's attic.

At breakfast the next morning, Anna took her usual seat closest to the window with a cup of tea in her hand. It was starting to rain, thick gray clouds rolling slowly in the sky above the hospital spilling fat, cold rain drops that streaked the windows and made everything in the asylum feel damp. The weather report was calling for mid morning thunderstorms with high winds, maybe even a bit of hail. It was a rather violent end to the winter as Anna looked forward to her second spring at Westborough.

Even as a child Anna had loved the rain, and thunderstorms especially. She liked waking to gloomy skies and low lying fog that hung over Buffalo like a funeral shroud. It wasn't that she was a particularly morbid person, she just enjoyed the feeling of being warm and protected in her room while Mother Nature raged outside. She had never been frightened of thunder. During a storm she would often creep out onto the screened in porch and watch the lightning forks split the sky as thunder rolled overhead. It was the only thing she and her father had ever shared; Malcolm would sit in his wicker rocker smoking a pipe while Anna curled up in the matching armchair. Together they would watch in complete silence, the only sound the rain rolling off the roof and off the leaves of the great oak trees in the front yard.

Rain in an asylum was something altogether different. Earlier that morning Anna had laid in bed listening to the drops hammer against the slate roof, pinging off the heavy metal window screens. When she had finally rolled out of bed and put her bare feet on the cold wood floor, she went right to the window and watched the storm break the surface of Lake Chauncy, little waves flooding back and forth and lapping at the shore. It was peaceful, watching the storm from so far off the ground.

The cafeteria was more crowded than usual; storms tended to drive people in where it was warm and Anna wasn't the only person cuddled up to a cup of something hot. Because of the storm there seemed to be an extra bit of electricity in the air as everyone wondered aloud just how bad it would get. It had been a mild winter without much snow and it seemed people were eager for some sort of weather related event, even if it was just a bit of hail.

Looking up Anna spotted Harper and gave her a quick wave. "Hey, how about this storm?" Harper shook the rain out of her hair and dried her hands on her lab coat. "Did you hear the latest?"

Anna shook her head. "No I didn't. Why?"

"This might turn into a hurricane according to the National Weather Service."

"You're kidding!" Eyes wide, Anna looked outside at the thickening clouds and shook her head in wonder. "This time of year? That's the strangest thing I have ever heard."

Harper nodded. "Apparently it's the remnants of a tropical storm down south that's sweeping up the coast."

Just as Harper finished speaking the ancient PA system crackled to life. "Attention staff and patients...attention please."

"Ha who knew that thing still worked!" Harper crowed, chuckling.

"With the approaching storm we are anticipating power outages. In case of a loss of power, all staff are asked to direct patients to the basement." Feedback ripped through the overhead speakers and everyone covered their ears.

"Apparently it doesn't work well," Anna complained, screwing her eyes shut.

The system buzzed again and the same disembodied voice crackled to life. "Again, in the event of an outage please direct patients to the basement. Make sure each patient is properly dressed and they are to bring a pillow and blanket. Main building occupants will shelter in the bowling alley. All wards will report to their assigned locations. Thank you."

"Well this should be fun." Rolling her eyes, Harper tied her hair back and wiped the moisture from her forehead. "Squeezing a few thousand people into the basement for God knows how long. Any chance you want to stick with me? Give me a hand?"

"Of course." It beat wandering around by herself and not knowing where she might be when the brunt of the storm hit. At least if she was with Harper she would know where to go.

Throughout the day the staff worked quickly to gather supplies and rush them to the basement. Canned food, condensed milk, and tins of crackers were stacked in each of the designated basement areas. Medications were collected and catalogued then stacked on carts that were sent down on the elevators. The staff would not be taking any chances.

Anna pitched in the best she could, gathering extra blankets and pillows, piling them in empty laundry carts and taking them down in the freight elevator. When the first lights began to flicker, Anna headed for the nurses' station to wait for Harper, but after twenty minutes Anna began to worry.

"Has anyone seen Dr. Westcott?"

A nurse passed by her with frightened eyes and shook her head. "No I haven't miss, but you should make your way down to the basement. Power has already gone out in two of the wards. The main building won't be far behind."

Wringing her hands, Anna scanned the passing crowds for Harper but she saw no sign of her. By the time Anna decided to head to the basement there was no one else around. She stopped for a moment to marvel at the sight of the wards completely emptied out, an eerie sight that could have been a portent of things to come.

Descending the stairs down into the basement, Anna felt the cold seeping into her bones and she realized she never grabbed anything for herself-- no blanket, no pillow, not even a jacket. All she had on was her jeans and a ratty old button down sweater she had filched from her aunt's closet before she left for college. Underground where the windows were set high up in the cinderblock walls there were a number of gas lanterns hanging from the pipes and someone had set up folding tables to hold bottles of water and extra emergency blankets. Some of the patients were milling around the tables, their anxiety etched on their faces. Others were whooping it up in the bowling alley, winging balls into the gutter and slapping one another on the back.

Anna threaded her way through the crowd searching for Harper but instead she found Peder, huddled at a corner table in the bowling alley with a book and a pen light. He had wrapped himself in a plaid blanket and he had a bottle of water balanced on his knee. Hoping he wouldn't notice her, Anna kept her head down and moved past the bowling alley and into the hallway that led to the wards. She was a few feet away from the tunnel entrance to the Kennedy School when she felt a hand clap over her mouth and an arm circled her shoulder. Suddenly she was being pushed and pulled down the tunnel, the light of a tiny flashlight bouncing off the pipes in front of her. At the other end of the tunnel was a door and her attacker let go of her momentarily to open it. She had just enough leverage to pull back and bite the hand that was over her mouth until she heard a grunt of pain.

"God damn you Anna!" Peder shined his light on his hand where Anna had left teeth marks in the soft, fleshy web between his thumb and index finger. "What did you do that for?"

Anna turned on him, hands balled into fists at her sides trying to decide whether or not to take a swing at him. "Are you kidding me?" Her voice echoed back at her through the tunnel, her words slapping her in the face as cold air rushed in from the basement of the school. "You just grabbed me and dragged me down a tunnel. What did you expect me to do?"

Peder lunged forward and pinned her against the wall, his breath hot on her cheek as his chest heaved with anger. "You told them I was still sleepwalking to that room."

"What?" Anna felt her mouth sag open in surprise. "What are you talking about?"

"I have someone watching my room around the clock now. I'm not allowed to go anywhere on my own because of you."

Shaking her head, Anna's heart pulsed with fear. "I didn't tell them anything. Harper said…"

"Harper said, Harper said…" Peder slammed his hand on the wall just above her head. "I don't care what that bitch doctor said. This is your fault. How else would they know every word of our conversations?"

"Even Harper doesn't know every word of our conversations!"

"I heard them," he growled, spittle collecting in the corners of his mouth. "I heard them talking about me, the psycho who believes in ghosts. They all knew about the handprint and the woman in the room."

It had to be his paranoia. She hadn't told anyone the specifics of their conversations, and even if she had told Harper the details she wouldn't have shared any of them with the orderlies. "Peder, you need to calm down. They don't know anything."

"Yes they do," he yelled, dragging his arm across his mouth to wipe away the moisture that had collected on his lips, then lowering his voice. "Yes they do. They're talking about me, all of them."

Sighing, Anna shook her head, unsure what to say to get Peder to relax. She was frightened but she also had a general understanding of what was happening in Peder's brain. He truly believed that everyone was talking about him, making fun of him. She was saved from figuring out what to say to him by a staff member in the Kennedy School who spotted the open door.

"Hey! You two! What are you doing in there?"

Anna broke away from Peder and ran as fast as she could down the tunnel, back to the main hospital. She fought her way through the warren of basement rooms until she finally found Harper manning one of the tables with bottled water. The storm was picking up speed, the wind rattling the glass in the window frames, pelting them with dime sized hail. "Harper thank God I finally found you." Anna bent at the waist, hands on her knees, trying to catch her breath.

"What's going on? What happened?" Harper put her hand on Anna's back and rubbed little circles on her spine.

"Peder, he dragged me into the tunnel that goes over to Kennedy. He thinks I told you all these things and that you told the orderlies," she sucked in a hard breath and coughed. "He thinks they're talking about him."

"Jesus." Harper blew out a sigh. "He's really falling apart. Did he hurt you?"

Anna shook her head, tears welling in her eyes. "No, he just scared me. I might have hurt him though. I kind of bit him in the hand." She didn't dare look up at Harper as she said it. She was mortified that she had done that to him but it had been instinctual to lash out.

After a beat Harper burst out laughing, loud guffaws that bounced off the soggy walls. "You bit him? Good for you!"

Soon Anna was laughing too, her fear and embarrassment forgotten. "I think I left a pretty good bruise too."

Harper slapped her hard on the back and wiped away tears of laughter as Anna wiped away tears of-- well, she didn't know what. Relief.

"I'll handle Peder in the morning. Right now, you stay close to me and let's weather this storm the best we can."

For the rest of the night Anna helped Harper hand out water as the thunder raged outside. It was close to three in the morning when the last patient had fallen asleep propped up in a chair just outside the bowling alley. Sinking to the floor, Harper twisted the top off a bottle of water and drank deeply, her head back and her eyes closed. "God I'm exhausted."

"Me too." Pushing her hair off her face, Anna looked out over the crowd of sleeping patients and searched for Peder but he was nowhere to be found.

"Dr. Westcott?" A young man with short brown hair and a collection of ballpoint pens in his shirt pocket leaned over the empty water table to get Harper's attention. "I believe I have one of your patients."

"What do you mean you have him?" She stood and brushed the basement dust off the seat of her pants. "Who are you?"

"I'm Edward Britton. I work at the Kennedy School." He must have been the voice on the other side of the tunnel door, the one who had allowed her to escape from Peder. He obviously hadn't seen her face in the tunnel; there wasn't even a flicker of recognition as he looked from her to Harper, then back again. "He was in the tunnel that leads from here to the school basement. I believe he was in there with a woman, though I don't know exactly what they were doing in there. I suppose I could guess…"

"I'll stop you right there Mr. Britton. Thank you for breaking it up and thank you for detaining him."

Edward nodded tersely and headed back to the tunnel as Harper covered her face with her hands. "Shit. Shit, shit double shit."

"What? What's wrong?"

Harper let out a long breath and looked down at Anna. "Now I'm going to have to write up a report about your little encounter in the tunnel."

"But why?"

"Someone else from a separate program is involved now. He knows Peder's name, knows he belongs over here. He'll likely report it."

"And if you don't write it up, it'll come down on you for not supervising your patients."

Harper nodded. "You got it."

"Shit," Anna agreed. "I'm sorry."

"Don't apologize. It's not your fault."

"Maybe it is. I pushed his buttons a bit too hard yesterday at the dispensary."

"That wasn't your fault either," Harper said gently, reaching out to pat Anna's shoulder. "Peder is self-destructing. You just happen to be in his path."

Anna looked over at Peder, his eyes closed, his chest softly rising and falling under his blanket. He looked so harmless, sleeping under the flickering gas lights. Leaning her head back against the wall, Anna fought to keep her eyes open, afraid to fall asleep now that Harper was distracted trying to fill out an incident report. It would only be a few more hours until the sun came up, then she could retreat back to her room and crawl into her own bed.

When the sun finally rose and the staff started waking the patients, Anna got to her feet and stretched her cold, stiff limbs. She watched as two male orderlies herded Peder and a couple of other patients out of the bowling alley and up the stairs, keeping Peder at arm's length in case he should cause another problem. Turning in the opposite direction, Anna climbed the stairs to the ward and grabbed a paper cup, filled it with water, and pulled her pills out of her pocket. She washed one down and went to sit on the couch in the day room so she could take a quick nap while the patients settled in.

Harper found Anna curled on the sofa, her arm flung over her face snoring softly. She felt Harper shake her awake and she sat up, rubbing the fog from her head. "Hey, shouldn't you be in your room, in your own warm, comfortable bed?"

"I figured I would stick around so I didn't waste the entire day."

Looking closely at her eyes, Harper took Anna by the chin and turned her face from one side to the other. "You came up here and took a pill didn't you?"

"I did. I didn't sleep at all last night. I figured I needed the rest."

"You need to take them on a schedule my dear. Same time every day. They're not there just to knock you out."

Anna nodded. "I know. I don't normally. It was just because of the storm last night."

Sighing, Harper dropped Anna's chin and stood to go. "Go get some sleep. We'll talk tomorrow."

Chapter 16

When Anna woke the next morning she felt unnaturally groggy, her brain slow and mushy. Picking up the bottle of pills, Anna couldn't remember when she had taken another pill. Had she taken more than one by accident? She slowly swung her legs over the side of the bed and put her feet on the floor, her legs feeling slightly rubbery. It took substantially longer than usual for her to shuffle to the bathroom where she ran herself a bath and filled it with bubbles. Maybe she was coming down with something. She would go later and see if she had a fever, but for now a good hot bath should do the trick. A folded towel made for a makeshift pillow and she propped the Maggie and Kate Fox book on her knees as she sank into the bubbles.

The heat from the water sank deep into her bones and her muscles relaxed, but as she lay there, she started to feel nauseous and dizzy. She must have taken one pill too many last night and now her stomach was rolling and her head felt fuzzy. It wasn't a good feeling.

When she finally got out of the water and wrapped herself in a towel, she had to sit on the edge of the tub to get her bearings. Once she was dressed Anna headed out to find Harper and tell her what was happening, but as she walked the halls searching for her friend, she felt as if the walls were closing in on her and she couldn't remember where she was going, or how to get to Harper. When she reached the ward, she stumbled and grabbed onto the counter outside the nurses' station to steady herself, but her hand slipped, pulling down a plastic rack filled with paperwork that clattered to the floor. Alice Lambert came out from behind the window to see what had happened and found Anna prostrate on the floor.

"Can we get a doctor here! Someone call Dr. Westcott!" Anna felt Nurse Lambert searching frantically for her pulse, lightly tapping Anna's cheek, trying to rouse her. Even though she could hear and feel everything going on around her, Anna just couldn't open her eyes. She felt strong hands circle her and lift her off the floor, then felt herself being carried. She could also hear Harper's voice, faint but clear, barking out orders.

"I think she's overdosed on Ativan. Get some charcoal."
Anna felt the soft give of a mattress under her and the blankets
being pulled up to her chin. Then she felt the cold shock of a tube
being put down her throat followed by a dose of charcoal. "Anna,
Anna can you hear me? You need to let the charcoal do its job."

Her reflexes were taking over and she was fighting against
the tube, trying to push it out of her mouth, but someone kept
pushing it back in. Finally she felt her stomach take one final roll
and she began to choke.

"Pull the tube! She's going to vomit. Pull the tube and grab
that trash can."

The moment the tube slid from her throat, she rolled onto
her side and vomited into her trashcan. She retched over and over
until she thought there was nothing left to throw up as Harper
rubbed her back and whispered her encouragement.

"There you go. That's a good girl. Just let it all out."

Exhausted, Anna collapsed onto her stomach and let her
head hang off the edge of the bed. Harper sat her up and put a
straw in her mouth. As Anna took a pull, she tasted the sweet cold
snap of ginger ale.

"That's it, drink it all honey." Harper's voice had been
replaced by Nurse Lambert's and Anna tried her best to finish the
entire cup of soda. As soon as she was finished, she dropped back

into the pile of pillows that had been arranged behind her head and let her eyes fall closed.

When she woke again, it was dark-- she had slept the entire day away and now her throat was killing her, her head pounding. She rolled over to find Harper sitting at her bedside, reading a magazine. "Morning sunshine."

"What time is it?"

Harper looked down at her watch. "It's nearly time for dinner. Think you can handle some soup?"

Anna nodded. "Harper, what happened?"

Sighing, Harper closed her magazine and leaned forward. "You took a few too many Ativan."

"How many is a few?"

"Two. It looks like when you got back to your room you took a pill, then woke in the middle of the night and took another. That means you took a total of three in a twelve hour span." Harper gave her a wry smile. "Technically an overdose."

"Oh god. I feel so stupid. I can't believe I did this and caused all this trouble."

Harper casually opened her magazine again and pretended to be focused on the pages. "Anna, is that what you think happened? That you accidentally took an extra pill?"

"Are you serious?" Anna sat bolt upright in bed and gawped at Harper. "Of course it was an accident. How could you even ask me that?"

Harper put up her hands in mock surrender. "Alright, alright." Turning away from Anna she went back to her page flipping, occasionally shooting her sideways glances. "Are you one hundred percent sure it was an accident?"

"Enough Harper! It was just an accident. Pure mistake."

"You would tell me if you were considering, you know..."

"Come on Harper. Of course I would talk to you."

Harper sighed and closed her magazine. "Ok fine. I'll take your word for it. But I'm going to keep an eye on you and on your medication."

"Fine. But it was just an accident." Harper said nothing as Anna huffed, her arms crossed over her chest. "I'm sorry I scared you."

"Damn right you did." She could tell Harper was trying not to smile. "You sit tight and I'm going to have some soup sent up. Do want tea?"

"Oh yes please!" Nodding eagerly, Anna sank back into her pillows as Nurse Lambert took Harper's place beside the bed. She pulled the covers up to her chin and closed her eyes, waiting for

Harper to come back with her food. She had never taken medication like that before and she had had no idea what to expect or how she would feel when they finally hit her. Sleep had been so elusive for so long that the feeling of drifting off so fully must have made her subconscious crave it to the point where she lost track of whether or not she had taken a pill. In spite of everything that had happened she had no intention of harming herself by abusing her medication and she hated to think that Harper would even imagine that to be a possibility.

Even when she had tried to sink into the pond at her aunt's she hadn't thought about dying; she had only thought about silence, what it might feel like to turn off every thought and every feeling. She just wanted her broken heart to stop hurting, for the water to rush in and fill the cracked spaces where the pain had gathered. It wasn't that she wanted to leave her life, she just wanted a moment's peace from it.

Somehow though, even the medication didn't stop the dreams. It tamped them down a bit, but after that first night of blissful blank sleep, she couldn't push them out of her mind completely. The last few nights, rather than wandering the old wards, she dreamed she was a patient, confined to one of the rooms on the female ward. The logical part of her mind knew that it was just stress; she had been thinking about her mother a lot lately, and her aunt. On top of that Anna was so tired that she was seeing things in that window, seeing her mother in that window.

Anna was disappointed when Harper delivered her tray with apologies; she wouldn't be able to stay and instead left Nurse Lambert sitting guard silently, her back rod straight in Anna's wooden desk chair. Alice didn't seem too eager to strike up a conversation so Anna finished her soup in silence, then rolled over to close her eyes. The next time she woke, she realized she hadn't moved an inch all night. The exhaustion of having that tube down her throat had pressed her down so deep that she could see the shape of her body, curled in a fetal position, molded into her mattress. Strange how her mattress looked far more worn, frayed than usual. Of course most days Anna woke in such a hurry that she barely noticed her surroundings. This was the first time in months that she had risen feeling as if she had actually rested. She rolled over and looked up at the ceiling, then glanced over at Alice, fast asleep in her chair with her chin resting on her chest..

She threw the covers aside and slowly climbed out of bed, realizing she had been tucked in fully clothed. Slipping into the bathroom, Anna reached down and washed her face, then ran a brush through her hair until it was smooth enough to tie back. She changed her clothes and brushed her teeth, then went back out into her room where Nurse Lambert snored softly. Her stomach rumbled and she decided to head down to the cafeteria; it was the first time in ages she had an appetite and she shuffled along with the other patients, heaping her plate with scrambled eggs and greasy bacon, the fixed herself a plastic mug of tea. The smell of the food was so thick, so heady that she nearly swooned inhaling its goodness.

Taking a seat in the corner of the cafeteria, Anna scanned the sea of faces for Peder but there was no sign of him. That was fine with her, she didn't have the energy to deal with another one of his outbursts. The next time she ran into him she wanted to have her wits about her and at that moment she still felt rather dull around the edges, almost like a hangover. She pressed her knuckles into her eyes and rubbed hard, then blinked as she looked around at the tables scattered around the tile floor, the serving counter in the middle of the room wreathed by the remains of the paper lanterns that had been hung for New Year's Eve. The windows were closed this morning and it was hard to see through the thick mesh to the courtyard outside but Anna knew that if she could see the window, way up at the top of the ward, there would be nothing there.

Polishing off the last of her breakfast, Anna wondered if she could get away with seconds, but thought better of it. She already felt a bit overstuffed, in fact when she looked down she realized she had filled out quite a bit since she had come to Westborough. Funny, she had been so busy over the last two years to even notice how much weight she had gained. She stood and carried her empty tray to the counter and downed the last of her tea before tossing the mug into the wash basin with her other dishes. Kitchen staff would come along and collect the wheeled cart filled with soapy dishes to be loaded into the massive industrial dishwashers in the back next to the cast iron stoves that had been in use since the day the hospital opened in 1848.

When she finally wandered back to her room, she was surprised to find Harper standing just inside her door with Nurse Lambert and two fairly beefy orderlies..

"Where the hell have you been?" Harper asked, genuine concern etched on her face. "I came in here to make sure you'd eaten last night and I found Nurse Lambert in here sawing away on the nose flute, keeping watch over your empty bed."

"I'm so sorry," Anna shrugged, palms up in confusion. "I slept like a rock for the first time in ages and I woke up starving. I went to get breakfast."

"I'm certainly glad to hear you slept well but you should be in bed." Harper jerked her head towards the bed. "Go."

"Yes ma'am."

"I also brought you a new medication." Harper pulled a giant sheet of pills out of a binder and waved it in front of her. "It's in a blister pack so you can clearly see how many you've taken. But just to be on the safe side, Nurse Lambert or I will be the one to give it to you."

Nodding, Anna began to feel embarrassed that Harper thought she needed adult supervision. "Harper, do you believe me that it was just an accident? That I didn't...overdose...on purpose?"

Harper pursed her lips and made a "hmm" sound, flipping open the binder and pretending to study it. "Let's talk later." Handing Anna a paper cup, she popped open the first bubble and handed the pill to Anna, watching her swallow it.

"Sure. Later." Anna nodded and climbed into bed, grabbing a book and settling in. It bothered her that Harper was being so cold and clinical with her, that she was suddenly being so professional with her. Anna could tell that Harper didn't quite believe her, that her protests about the pills were falling on deaf ears. It broke her heart to think that Harper doubted her even in the least. She was so distracted that she had read the same sentence at least twenty times without even knowing what it was she was reading. Her eyelids were feeling heavy, her mouth fuzzy. She drifted off again, began to dream.

In her dreams the hospital was darker, shabbier than usual. The furniture frayed around the edges and the tile floor was chipped in more places than it should be. Cobwebs hung from the ceiling and dust collected on nearly every surface, even the ones Anna remembered cleaning that very morning. The dream was so vivid that Anna could feel herself wandering the halls, she could hear her footsteps echoing in her ears as she walked along, her heels clicking. She looked down and she was wearing the chunky brown lace up boots she had been wearing that night in Niagara Falls.

As she tripped down the hallway that connected the rest of the hospital to the old isolation wards, the concrete sun porches that overlooked the maintenance buildings, the floor changed from tile to cracked concrete and as she walked, the walls disappeared and in their place, wild branches with dark green leaves and razor sharp thorns. "Rose bushes. Rose bushes, she said she saw roses and she thought of me. Mother! Mother where are you?"

Then she was running, running through the warm night air, sweat pouring down her spine, her hair plastered to her forehead. When she reached up to push it out of her eyes she realized she had bangs, thick ones, and her hair was short. Looking down, she was wearing a summer dress and those boots, the brown boots that her mother always said reminded her of a lady's Victorian riding boots. How she had loved those boots. As she ran, the rose bushes began to reach out and twine around her ankles, thorns piercing her boots and digging into her skin. She cried out in pain, over and over, until she felt a hand on her shoulder shaking her awake.

"Jesus Anna. Wake up!" Harper was standing over her, shaking her and slapping her cheek. "Anna come on. You're having a nightmare. You need to wake up."

Anna's eyes focused on Harper's face, crimson with fear and agitation. "I'm awake. I'm fine." She struggled to sit up, gripping Harper's hand as she pulled herself to a sitting position.

"You were yelling for your mother," Harper said softly, helping Anna situate herself, propping pillows behind her to make her more comfortable.

"Rose Bushes."

"What?"

Anna sighed and looked over at Harper. "The first time I dreamed about her being in that room she tried to tell me something about rosebushes. Just now when I was having that nightmare, I was back in Niagara Falls, the night she died, walking down the sidewalk. And it was lined with rosebushes."

"Listen, Anna. I'm really sorry I came down on you so hard. I'm just worried about you." She tucked her hands in the pockets of her lab coat and cocked her head to the side, waiting for Anna to say everything would be okay. "You've been dreaming about your mother a lot. Are you remembering more about the night she died?"

Anna nodded, then shook her head. "I don't know. Sometimes I think I am, but other times I wonder if it's just my mind playing tricks on me."

"I'm so sorry. I can't even imagine how that feels, the not knowing. I honestly hoped the medication would help. I'm responsible for you and I can't seem to help you."

"You're responsible for me?"

"No, I said I *feel* responsible for you," she corrected. "I'm your friend. I want you to remember so you can move on. Sometimes I think if you had some answers..."

"You can't think like that. It's been more than a decade since she died and now my dad is gone too. There's no one left to ask."

Harper didn't argue, but Anna could see that she didn't agree with her and it broke her heart. Harper was the first woman she had connected with since leaving her Aunt Sarah for college. Making friends as an adult, especially a shy one with a healthy dose of social anxiety, terrified her beyond reason. Harper's effusive style and bold approach to socializing had made it far easier for Anna to fall into a friendship with her and now it was being overshadowed by talk of nightmares, death, and medication. It was exactly what Anna didn't want.

Chapter 17

Over the next few days Anna could feel the gulf between herself and Harper widening. She visited less and less each day, leaving Alice Lambert to sit silent vigil at Anna's bedside. When she finally woke one morning to find her prison guard gone, she slipped out to the banks of the lake and sat at the edge, enjoying the first teasing breaths of spring that crept through the trees, chasing away the last of the winter chill. Anna sat wrapped in a wool blanket she had taken from the foot of her bed. As she sat, gazing out at the other shore, a shadow fell over her; she looked up, shielding her eyes, to find Peder standing over her.

"You look like hell."

. "It's been a rough week."

Peder looked around, then settled in next to Anna. "Tell me about your week darling." Putting on a fake British accent, he pretended to tip an imaginary cap in her direction. "There's a nasty rumor going around that you tried to off yourself."

"I did not." Anna glared at him but saw that behind the sarcasm there was genuine concern, so she told him everything-- the continued nightmares, her near death experience, the new medication. "I don't feel like myself. It's only been a few days of taking it but I feel like I'm in a bubble."

"Maybe you just need more time to adjust."

"Are you kidding?" She looked up at him, shocked, only to find he had said it with a straight face. "My God. You're serious. You think I need medication."

Peder shrugged. "Well I think you should give it a chance to do its job, see if it might help. The side effects might go away after a little while and then you'll find that they help."

She couldn't believe what she was hearing-- Peder condoning the use of medication to dull her senses. "You of all people. I thought you would understand not wanting to feel your senses dulled."

"Anna, you're not sleeping, and you're having vivid, frightening nightmares that are derailing your entire body system. You're seeing things in the old ward, just like I am."

"I'm not hallucinating, I'm dreaming," she argued. "And it's not like I'm hearing voices Peder. I just have bad dreams."

Peder looked at her, hard. "Why would you bring up hearing voices?"

"Well," Anna shrugged. "Because you know how dangerous that could be. You know that's the sign that something is really wrong." She very pointedly addressed this to him so that there was no doubt what she meant-- *there's a big difference between you and me. You're crazy, I'm not.* "And since that's not happening to me, I don't see what the major issue is if I don't want to keep taking medication."

Of all people she expected Peder to be sympathetic. He was loaded to the gills with medication; she saw the slight tremor in his hands when he reached for things, noticed how slowly and deliberately he moved and spoke. It kept him from seeing and hearing things but, Anna could see it made him sluggish and dull. It made her wonder, as she studied his admittedly handsome face, what he had been like in the days before his illness had destroyed him.

"I do understand," he said quietly. "But I also know that you need to get back to yourself and if it takes medication to do that…"

She couldn't even look at him, she was so disappointed. Here she was, softening in her resolve to remain unaffected by him, trying her best to see the man behind the insanity, and instead he takes Harper's side, tells her that she needs to be medicated when all she needs is to forget. "You yourself just said I look like hell. The drugs are doing that to me. I looked in the mirror this morning, I know I look like the walking dead."

"No you don't." Peder followed her gazed out to the opposite shore, watching the water pool around rocks that had risen to the surface, watching little rings spread where fish broke the water to feed. "You're still beautiful." He turned to look at her and frowned. "I'm sorry about what happened the night of the storm, in the tunnel."

Though she wasn't certain she was ready to forgive him for frightening her the way he did, she appreciated that he was apologizing. "You need to understand that there can never be anything between us."

Peder looked at her so intently that she had to turn away, but as she did he caught her chin gently in his hands. "You can't mean that Anna."

She did mean it; or at least she thought she meant it but now, with his fingertips resting on her chin and his eyes locked on hers, she could almost ignore where they were, though she couldn't quite forget what he was. "It's too dangerous Peder. You're sick."

"I know I let my temper get the better of me but I would never hurt you, I swear it. And the medication helps, I promise it does." He let his fingers slip from her chin, bringing his palms to her cheek. WIth his other hand he gently brushed her hair out of her eyes and pulled her closer.

Everything inside of her was telling her to push him away but she couldn't. Instead she found herself wrapping her knuckles in the fabric of his shirt as his lips touched hers. It only lasted a moment before he broke away but the electricity that surged through her brain pulsed long after he had ended the kiss. "I told you I knew all about you Anna Gilman." With that he stood and took off for the hospital, leaving Anna to wonder how long it would be before she regretted that kiss, but for the moment she would sit there just a little longer, enjoying the tingle in her lips. She sat with her arms wrapped around her knees until what little warmth the day had conjured slipped away and she began to shiver.

Heading slowly up the hill Anna spotted Harper coming from the other direction. She hurried her step and caught up to Anna just as she reached to open the door. "What are you doing out here?"

Anna shrugged. "I felt fine when I got up and Nurse Lambert wasn't there so I came out for a walk."

"You're adjusting to new medication, you have no idea how it'll affect you. You should be in bed."

Letting out a derisive snort she muttered, "I know exactly how it's going to make me feel."

"What was that?" Harper narrowed her eyes as Anna puffed out her chest and readied herself for an argument.

"I said, it makes me feel like my tongue is swollen and my head is a helium balloon, barely even attached."

"Exactly why you shouldn't be out here, down by the lake." Harper grabbed Anna's elbow and began to drag her towards the front door. "I'm walking you back to your room. You need rest."

"What are you doing? My room is in Paine Hall."

Harper didn't answer her but Anna was fairly certain she saw her roll her eyes as she pulled harder on Anna's elbow. "Let's go Anna."

Dragging her along, Harper frog marched Anna up the stairs and into the female wing where she opened a door and ushered Anna in. She was surprised to see her pile of library books stacked neatly next to the bed, her clothes hanging in the closet, and the bed crisply made with her own blankets. "When did you do this? Who moved all my things?"

"It's better for you this way Anna. You need some time."

"Time for what?" But Harper didn't answer, didn't even look back as she walked out and shut the door behind her. Moments later one of the younger nurses knocked on the door and handed her a pill along with a paper cup full of water.

"I'm not taking this."

The angelic blond nurse's face turned to stone and she pushed the pill into Anna's hand. "Miss Gilman, you will take your medication or it will be given to you by other means."

"Other means?" Anna shouted. "What are you going to do, hold me down and shove it down my throat?"

"This medication," the nurse said, glancing at Anna's open palm. "Can also be injected. I hear it's a painful one though," she snickered, raising her eyebrows as Anna took the pill and swallowed it.

Looking around in disbelief, Anna realized that all of her belongings had been painstakingly moved from the nurses' dorm to a patient room, everything put back exactly the way it had been in Paine Hall. When had this happened? When she was talking to Peder? She lay down in bed and stared up at the ceiling, silently counting the cracks in the plaster that spidered out from the overhead light. As she stared, her limbs began to feel heavy and her head full. She closed her eyes and dropped off into a black and dreamless state that was somewhere deeper than sleep. When she woke again it was dark outside and it took her quite some time to orient herself, looking around at the unfamiliar walls that she felt like she had seen a hundred times before but couldn't place.

Her stomach growled as a sharp knock on her door jolted her out of bed. Pulling a cardigan close over her pajamas, Anna opened the door a fraction to find Harper standing there with a tray of food in her hand. "You missed pretty much every meal today." She raised the tray so Anna could see that it was laden with roast beef, mashed potatoes, and stuffing swimming in gravy.

Reaching out, Anna took the tray from Harper and held the door open for her to come in. "What do you mean every meal? I ate breakfast this morning."

Anna offered Harper the only chair and sat cross legged on the bed with the tray balanced on her knees while she ate. "Anna, it's Friday. You haven't eaten since yesterday morning."

How had she lost an entire day? Was that new medicine that strong? Harper watched her eat, but Anna was so hungry it hardly bothered her. When she was finished she handed Harper the empty tray and sat back against the head of her bed.

"Thank you for that."

Harper nodded and said, "You're welcome. Now, I know you don't want to talk about things but I think we need to."

"I should have known you would want to talk."

"Anna, you're important to me and so is your health. You're not improving."

Shrugging, Anna tried her best to dismiss Harper's concern. "So I'm a little out of it. What difference does that make?"

"It's more than that Anna. Twice I've had to change your medications and somehow you're still having nightmares and you're still hallucinating."

Anna sat upright and narrowed her eyes at Harper. "What do you mean hallucinating?"

Harper made a sound in her throat. "The woman in the window, your mother."

"That's not a hallucination Harper. That was just my imagination playing tricks on me."

"No it's not Anna." Sighing, Harper reached out and patted Anna's hand before she yanked it away angrily. "My point is you need to take advantage of the resources that are being offered to you. This has gone far beyond just a few nightmares." Harper leaned forward in her chair and rested her elbows on her knees. She looked at the floor as she spoke. "You're a full blown insomniac. Without the medications your dreams border on night terrors. The visions are carrying over into your waking hours and you're hallucinating. The lack of sleep is making you jumpy, paranoid, and not the tiniest bit touchy."

"What are you saying Harper? Are you saying I need therapy? Or that I need more medication? Because that's not going to happen."

"Anna, I don't think you have a choice."

"I sure as hell do have a choice. Get out."

Harper looked up, surprised. "What?"

"I said, get out. Get. Out."

Anna pointed towards the door and waited for Harper to leave. "Anna, come on. You can't throw me out like this."

"Like hell I can't," she said, climbing out of bed and throwing the door open. "It's my room. I can throw you out if I damn well please."

"I'll just come back," Harper spat as Anna tried to close the door on her.

"Thanks for the warning," Anna growled, closing the door the rest of the way and leaning her hip against it. "Don't expect me to open the door to you."

She waited until she could no longer hear Harper's angry footsteps in the hallway, then climbed back into bed and pulled the covers up over her head, but then she began to feel silly so she sat up to grab a book. It wasn't long before her eyes would no longer focus on the page and she felt herself drift back into that strange marshmallow feeling sleep that seemed to be manufactured by her medication, that ethereal cushion that allowed her brain to slide into oblivion. And this time she didn't care when she woke up again. If she woke up again.

Chapter 18

Anna found herself wanting to talk to Valerie, someone
unbiased who would listen to her without judging her mental state,
but after her confrontation with Harper, Anna was reluctant to try
to leave her room in case they should run into each other. It
seemed though that apparently Harper's threat to return was an
empty one; the next person to knock on the door was Alice
Lambert with a dinner tray in her hand. "I see Harper feels bad
about the way she treated me earlier." Alice didn't say anything,
just handed Anna the tray with a small smile while she backed out
of the room.

Finally, after four days of eating her meals in her room, Anna
ventured to the bathroom with her robe slung over her arm. She
had been cooped up so long that she was beginning to smell rather

ripe, her hair greasy and stringy. Stepping into the shower, she cranked the hot water as high as it would go without scalding her. She worked shampoo through her matted hair and scrubbed her face until it was nearly raw, then wrapped herself in her towel. Using her hand to wipe the steam from the mirror, Anna leaned in close to inspect her face. Her eyes still looked a little glassy but not nearly as wild as they had the past few days. Maybe she was finally getting back to normal.

Anna stood in the doorway of her room and surveyed the mess that had taken over. "I have to clean this up," she muttered as she pushed the pile of trays out into the hallway for maintenance to take care of. Once she was dressed she grabbed her trash can and went around picking up used tissues, empty prescription bottles, and crumpled napkins. She stacked her books back where they belonged and straightened up the top of her bureau. Carrying her dirty laundry, she headed down the stairs to the basement and threw her clothes in the washing machine.

It had been a long week, one that made her wonder if the medication was still a good idea since it obviously made her into someone even she didn't recognize. Maybe if she talked to Harper calmly about stopping the medication, and maybe apologize to her friend for her behavior, Harper would listen but when she got to the ward, she was nowhere to be found. Heading for Harper's office, Anna got as far as the main stairs when Alice Lambert stepped in front of her.

"What are you doing?" Anna barked, sidestepping the young nurse.

Alice jumped and moved with her, continuing to block her way to the stairs. "You're not to leave the ward Miss Gilman."

"What do you mean I can't leave the ward? Get out of my way!"

"I'm sorry Miss Gilman." Alice spread her hands in a classic maneuver that was meant to calm. "I'm just following Dr. Westcott's orders."

"Well I'm telling you to buzz off. I'm going to find Dr. Westcott myself."

When Alice didn't move, Anna began to raise her voice, growling at her to get out of the way. Her voice must have carried far enough to attract attention as all motion ceased in the day room and staff gathered to watch the standoff happening at the top of the stairs. Out of the corner of her eye Anna spotted Peder hovering at the back of the group, watching her carefully through eyes narrowed to slits. Next thing she knew, Harper was at her side, grabbing at her elbow.

"Anna, come on. I've got her Nurse Lambert." Alice nodded and stepped aside, heading back to the ward to help clear the day room of curious rubberneckers. "Come with me to my office."

Anna resisted but Harper dug her fingers deeper into the soft flesh of Anna's arm.

Harper led Anna down the hall to her office and pushed her down onto the couch. She went straight to the coffee maker and poured a cup, then added some sugar and handed it to Anna. "Here, drink up and take a breath."

"You know I hate coffee."

"I don't care. Drink it." She commanded sharply.

Anna slugged down the coffee and handed the cup back to Harper who had perched on the arm of the couch Anna was sitting on. She ran her hands over the soft butter leather while she waited for whatever lecture Harper was about to throw her way.

"You're not allowed off the ward Anna," she said quietly. "They've taken away your privileges."

She shook her head no, as if that might make Harper go away. "They can't do that."

"They can, and they did. They don't think you can be trusted any longer and there are plenty of others who like to have the freedom you've had for the past year. I'm sorry."

Anna looked up, confused by what Harper was saying. "Freedom? What are you talking about? I'm a professional."

"No, you're not Anna." She suddenly noticed that Harper was studiously avoiding making eye contact with her. She looked up at the ceiling and twisted her fingers in her lap. "I'm referring you to Dr. Brown."

"Why would you do that Harper?" Sliding away, Anna looked up with hate in her eyes. "Why would you do that?"

"You need to talk to someone and it can't be me anymore."

Anna stood and folded her hands primly in front of her. "You have a lot of nerve Harper. You're supposed to be my friend, but instead you rat me out to Brown of all people."

"I didn't rat you out," Harper sighed. "Brown is my boss and he supervises my cases. He's here for me to lean on when I can't seem to break through to someone." She looked meaningfully at Anna. "I can't get through to you Anna."

"Get through to me about what?"

"You're not well Anna." Harper rose from the arm of the couch and took a step toward Anna. "You need to admit that and you need to accept help."

Anna stepped back and crossed her arms over her chest. "I don't need help. I'm fine." As she backed away, Valerie appeared in the doorway. "Valerie! Thank god. Tell her I'm fine!"

"Dr. Westcott, would you excuse us for a moment?"

Harper nodded and stepped out of the office, closing the door behind her. Valerie sat down on the couch and patted the empty space next to her, urging Anna to sit with her. Once she was seated, Valerie took a deep breath and reached out for Anna's hand.

"Do you remember what I said about not settling in here?"

Anna nodded. Of course she remembered. It was the oddest, most striking piece of advice Valerie had given her.

"And do you remember how I told you to use your journal to get to know yourself?"

Anna nodded again as Valerie drew a leather bound book from behind her back. It took Anna a moment to realize it was her journal that Valerie was holding and she was about to open it. "Where did you get that?"

"Dr. Westcott turned it over to me two days ago and I've read through most of it." She looked up from the pages she was flipping and looked at Anna with an expression she couldn't read. "I owe you an apology Anna."

"An apology for what?"

Valerie sighed and patted the back of Anna's hand. "For not getting involved sooner. Now that I have a better handle on what's going on with you, I realize I didn't check in with you often enough." Turning the journal around, she slid it onto Anna's lap and pointed to an entry in the middle. "Read that."

Glancing over the entry, Anna had a hard time deciphering the handwriting. "I didn't write this."

"Yes you did." Valerie pointed at the date. "You wrote it a week ago, just before Dr. Westcott changed your medication. You wrote that you believe your mother has come back from the dead to tell you something about her death, that you see her in the old wards."

"Well that's true, but it was just a dream."

"Anna, do you remember what happened the other night?"

"What are you talking about Valerie?"

"We found you in a patient room in the old ward talking to someone. When the orderly asked you who you were talking to, you told him you were talking to your mother and she was trying to tell you something about roses."

Tears welled in Anna's eyes and her throat began to close.

"You don't remember do you." Valerie watched as tears spilled down Anna's cheeks and she began to sob.

"It was just a dream. I know it was."

Valerie waited while Anna cried herself until she was empty of tears. "I think it's time we talked about your mother's death in more detail. Harper suspects you're remembering more details about that night and it's important that we explore that."

Anna shook her head fiercely. "No Valerie, I'll be fine. I don't want to talk about it." She swiped at her eyes with her sleeves and sniffed. "It was all just a dream, it's just stress."

"It's far more than stress Anna and you need to face that." Valerie motioned to two men who had appeared in the doorway.

"What are they doing here?" They were orderlies from her ward, one tall and strong with red hair and a beard, the other shorter and beefier with dark hair and glasses.

"They're here to escort you to Dr. Brown's office." Valerie dipped her chin and one of the orderlies stepped forward to help Anna up from the couch but she was too quick for him. She stood and darted past him, lurching towards the door, but the second orderly was ready for her and he lifted her off the ground, pinning her against his massive chest.

"Let me go! Put me down you monster!" She didn't even care that she was making a scene. There were other orderlies out in the hallway, other clinical staff, but she didn't care. She kicked her feet and whipped her head back and forth, trying to force him to put her down. "Get your hands off me!" She felt a hand snake up and clamp down over her mouth as the second orderly grabbed hold of her feet and tucked her ankles under his arm. Pulling a syringe out of his pocket, he uncapped it and jabbed it into Anna's arm, watching intently as the clear liquid inside the hypodermic passed into her veins.

When she woke again she was back in her room. She tried to sit up but found that she couldn't move her arms or legs. Looking down, she realized that she was restrained, leather cuffs buckled around her wrists and ankles. Panic overtook her and she began to thrash and to scream. An orderly appeared at her door then rushed into the room with a needle, and moments later she felt the heat of an injection in her arm and her eyes began to close.

Part II

Chapter 19

The night her mother died they had gone to dinner at a fancy restaurant, that's why she had been wearing her navy flowered dress with her favorite boots. There had been a small set-to in the hotel room when her father had tried to tell her to change; he said the boots looked ridiculous and he wouldn't be seen with her in a nice restaurant looking like she belonged on a horse farm. When Anna's bottom lip began to tremble, her mother had stepped in and yelled at her father to back off.

"Who cares what shoes she's wearing Malcolm?" she shouted, waving her hands at him. "Look at the way the rest of the world's teenagers dress and be grateful that your daughter doesn't look like a hooker."

"So it's better that she looks like a poor farm hand?" her father had snapped.

Sighing her mother turned and winked at her. "Malcolm, we are trying to teach our daughter to be herself which is a very difficult thing to do when you're a teenage girl. Having her father ridicule her fashion choices doesn't help her develop self-confidence." She smiled sweetly at her husband and batted her eyes.

Malcolm was powerless against his wife when she smiled. "Fine. She can wear the shoes." He turned to Anna. "But you will behave at dinner. None of your antics," he said, wagging his finger at her like she was a naughty toddler.

At the restaurant Anna had tried to order a Shirley Temple, her favorite drink that made her feel like an adult even though it was non-alcoholic, but her father immediately vetoed her choice. "You'll get a glass of soda water like a lady." Then he turned to the waiter and said, "She'll have a soda water."

Anna sulked but said nothing, having promised to behave, but she also resolved to say nothing at all to her father for the rest of the meal, even if he directed conversation her way. Sinking low in her seat, she hid her face behind the menu and tried to decide what she wanted for dinner but she realized all of the menu items were in French. As she reached over to tap her mother on the arm, her father noticed and shot her a look that could have chilled ice.

"What do you need sweetheart?" her mother asked, missing the look in her father's eye, or perhaps simply ignoring it.

"I don't know what these words are." As she pointed to the menu, the waiter returned to take their order.

Her mother politely told the waiter her order and began to lean in to help Anna when her father interrupted. "I'll have the veal and my daughter will have the duck." Snatching the menus from her mother, he snapped them shut and handed them to the waiter who was looking rather shell shocked at his speedy dismissal along with the dismayed look on 14-year-old Anna's face.

"But dad, I don't like duck."

"You've never even had duck," he snapped without even looking at her.

"I wanted something with chicken in it. And spaghetti."

"Duck is just like chicken," he sighed, exasperated with Anna's arguing. "And they don't have spaghetti here."

"Malcolm, why couldn't you have asked her what she wanted?" her mother demanded quietly. "She's not going to like the duck."

"Duck is good. It's much better than chicken."

Her mother rolled her eyes. "Malcolm, I don't like duck either and just because it's more expensive than chicken doesn't make it better."

Anna's head swiveled back and forth between her parents as they argued, hoping it wouldn't turn into one of their loud, ugly fights right here in the restaurant. The thought of being embarrassed by her parents' yelling in a fancy restaurant horrified her. "It's fine. I'll try the duck."

Her mother leaned towards her and said, "You don't have to try it just because your father is forcing you to."

"It's fine mom. Just don't argue ok?"

Sitting up, her mother glared at her father who was studying the label on the bottle of wine he had ordered. "I'm not the one arguing."

"You most certainly are the one arguing Teresa," her father retorted without taking his eyes off the bottle. "She said she'll eat the duck. Why can't you just leave it alone?"

"Because she doesn't want the duck!" Her mother's sharp voice carried over the restaurant and heads turned in their direction.

"Mother, stop it!" Anna hissed, slipping lower in her chair. "People are staring!"

"Yes, Teresa," Malcolm mocked. "Stop it. You're embarrassing your daughter."

Teresa let out a bark of laughter. "No Malcolm," she spat. "You're the one embarrassing her by not letting her order her own food like she's some kind of imbecile."

"Stop it!" This time Anna yelled to be heard over her parents. A man in a black jacket and slacks with a tight black bowtie left the podium at the front of the restaurant and approached their table. Anna knew she had gotten them in trouble so she pushed back her chair and bolted past the maitre'd and out the front door of the restaurant, running down the sidewalk and into the unfamiliar night. She had no idea if her parents would bother to come after her and she frankly didn't care. Besides, they were probably far more concerned with mollifying the restaurant's manager after their daughter's outburst. She didn't even want to think about it, she just wanted to get as far away from the arguing as possible.

Anna hurried down the main road, wandering in and out of the souvenir shops, watching as the crowds on the streets grew thinner, the night sky darker, and she suddenly needed to know just how late it was. And she wondered if her parents were finally out looking for her, thinking maybe it was time to make her way back to the hotel so they could stop worrying, but she had lost her bearings and couldn't remember which way the hotel was. She stepped out onto the sidewalk and looked up, wondering if maybe she would recognize some of the buildings but nothing looked familiar. Finally she saw a policeman striding toward her and she put out her hand to stop him.

"Excuse me, I'm lost."

The policeman looked down at her and smiled kindly. "What's your name young lady?"

"Anna Gilman. I'm staying in one of the hotels with my mother and father."

A shadow passed over his face and he bent lower. "What are your parents' names sweetie?"

"Malcolm and Teresa."

He looked sad as he reached out and took her hand. "I know just where to take you."

They walked a few blocks in silence until they reached the hotel and Anna jumped for joy when she recognized the front door of the fancy, expensive place with the name she couldn't pronounce. "Thank you so much! I know where I'm going now."

"Actually I think I'll walk you all the way up if that's ok." He led her to the elevator and pressed the button for her floor and when they stepped off she could see that there were more policemen standing outside their room. Her parents had been worried after all. Anna blew out a sigh of relief, ready to run in and apologize to her father for making a scene, but when she rushed into the room her father turned towards her with a look of such hatred and venom that it stopped her in her tracks.

"Get her out of her," he barked, pointing to the bedroom off the main living space in the suite. The policeman took her hand once again and led her into her room.

"Why don't you sit Anna," he said, crouching down in front of her once she was seated in the cushioned dressing chair. "My name is Michael by the way." He stuck out his hand for her to shake, just like a grown up would with another grown up. "How old are you Anna?"

"I just turned 14 two weeks ago."

"That's great. Happy Birthday! Listen…" he stopped and wrinkled his nose like he smelled something bad, then fixed his eyes on the carpet. "Something bad happened to your mom. She's been hurt."

"What do you mean hurt?" Anna could tell he was struggling to find a way to tell her which made her not want to hear what he had to say.

"Well, you see she…"

"Get out of here. Now." Malcolm stood in the doorway, his arms crossed over his chest, glaring at the officer. "This is a family matter and I'll deal with my daughter myself."

"Sir, with all due respect, you might want to control your anger before you talk with her."

"While I appreciate your professional parenting advice," he said, his voice dripping with sarcasm, "I think I'll handle my daughter how I see fit. Now leave before I report you to your supervisor."

With one final glance at Anna, the officer stood, tipped his cap at Malcolm, and walked out the door leaving Anna alone with her father who was seething with rage, so angry that he couldn't seem to form words.

"Daddy, what happened? He said mom was hurt?"

Malcolm lunged forward and grabbed Anna by the front of her dress, a tiny ripping noise twisting itself around his fingers. "Do you have any idea what you've done?"

Anna could only shake her head no as her father nearly lifted her off her chair with his anger.

"Your mother is dead. She's dead and it's your fault, you caused this. Mark my words, the moment your mother is in the ground, I will bury you too." He shook her hard until her head jerked forward, her teeth smashing together. "I never even wanted you, you know." He pushed her back against the chair and spit at her feet, then left the room, the door slamming behind him.

He remained true to his word, shipping her off the moment the last shovelful of dirt covered her mother's coffin. Anna's burial was merely a metaphor; her father believed that he had ended her life by separating her from him, from her childhood home, but in truth he had done the opposite; he had given her a new beginning. She had a new home where she would never have to listen to the sounds of her parents screaming obscenities at one another, she would never again hear her father call her mother crazy, would never hear her mother sobbing on the floor of the master bedroom as her father railed at her to control her horrid wench of a daughter.

Her aunt never raised her voice no matter how difficult Anna had been; and she had certainly been a hand full. After the incident with the pond Sarah insisted on taking Anna to a doctor, someone to talk to she explained, to help her get over her mother's death. The doctor her aunt had chosen was young, younger than any psychiatrist had a right to be in her opinion, but she came highly recommended and she was kind to Anna, gentle in her questioning. Though it made her slightly uncomfortable, when the doctor asked Sarah to step outside so she could talk to Anna alone, she agreed and gave her the space she knew she needed.

When the doctor was finished she left Anna in her office and stepped into the hallway to talk to Sarah. "It's my opinion," she said quietly but firmly, "that Anna is suffering from some acute post-traumatic stress."

Her aunt nodded. "I expected as much."

"That's not all. Anna's test results are a little concerning." She flipped open a folder and flipped through the papers. "I believe your niece also suffers from what we used to call manic depression."

"Bipolar?"

The doctor nodded. "And I think she's had it for a number of years. It would explain the mood swings you say her father complained about. And judging by what you've both told me about her father, I believe he may have suffered from it as well."

They left the office with a pile of pamphlets about Bipolar and a stack of prescriptions to fill. Anna's medications simply became a part of the daily routine in her aunt's house; Sarah didn't make a big deal about it, though she did tell Anna that if she started to feel worse or felt like she might want to hurt herself more than usual, she needed to let her know.

It took months for Anna to adjust to the heavy doses of antipsychotics and antianxiety medications. She hated how they made her feel, fat and slow. When she talked, she had difficulty remembering words and making her thoughts make sense. It took everything she had to get out of bed in the morning but her aunt was her constant cheerleader.

"Let's make a deal," she said one morning, sitting on the edge of Anna's bed. "You get one mental health day a week. It can be a day off from school, or a day off from chores here in the house."

Anna rolled over and looked at her aunt to see if she was joking but she was completely serious. She could play hooky? Or duck out of chores?

"The only rule is that you tell me why you need the mental health day and you give me fifteen minutes to talk about it." Sarah held her hand out for Anna to shake as if they were making a very serious deal, though Anna supposed that was exactly what they were doing.

Their agreement helped Anna finish high school without exceeding the prescribed number of absences. Sarah managed to get a few of them excused once she had predicted Anna's cycle of ups and downs and was able to schedule appointments on some of the days that Anna stayed home. Somehow it was easier for her to get out of bed for a doctor's appointment than for school. Then again, she didn't have to make much of an effort to hide her depression if she was going to the doctor.

By the fall of her senior year Anna had adjusted to her medications and managed to cash in on fewer and fewer of her mental health days to the point where she started making the honor roll. Her guidance counselor even called her in to talk about college.

"I hadn't thought about it," Anna shrugged.

"Do you have any thoughts as to what you'd like to do after you graduated?

She shrugged again. "I hadn't thought about that either actually."

"Well," her counselor flipped through Anna's file and smiled. "What about psychology?"

"Does that mean being a therapist?"

Mrs. Giordano nodded. "It could, or it could mean becoming a nurse in a psychiatric facility, or an occupational therapist. Maybe an art therapist if you like to draw. Do you like to draw?"

Anna shook her head. "I've never been very good at it."

"Oh you don't have to be good at it to be an art therapist. You just have to love art."

"I think I like the idea of being a nurse. I like helping people."

"That's wonderful! With your grades I think you'd be a great fit for SUNY Buffalo State. They have a great program." Turning in her chair, Mrs. Giordano grabbed a folder of information in the school's colors, black and orange with a tiger emblazoned on the front. "Think about it and let me know what you think."

Taking the folder, Anna tucked it carefully into her backpack and accepted a late pass to History. When she got home, she showed Sarah the folder and asked her if she thought college was something she could do.

"Of course. You could live here and commute. We could arrange your classes so you have a built in mental health day."

"Do you think it would be that easy?"

Sarah nodded, smiling while she bustled around the kitchen getting dinner together. "Of course it would. We can do it together."

And so Anna took her SATs and scored in the top percentile, then applied early for admission to SUNY Buff State in their psychology program as a commuter. She and Sarah sat at the kitchen table and poured over the class offerings, trying to fit in all the required courses while still having a free day. The first day of classes, Sarah dressed as "hip" as she could and walked to classes with Anna, hoping she blended in enough to not embarrass her niece. She could see that Anna was struggling to keep her anxiety in check but as Sarah watched her she could see a bit of a spark in her, something that told her she was going to be just fine.

Anna took to her studies like a fish to water, and she rose to the top of her class. After her first successful semester, she asked her aunt to help her find a way to take seven classes instead of five with an eye to graduating early. She immersed herself in the readings of Freud and Jung, but also excelled at writing and literary criticism-- college was the beginning of her love of books. It was also the first time she considered moving out of Sarah's house. One of her professors suggested a graduate program for psychiatric nursing, a competitive program that accepted only the best of the best, but it was in Massachusetts.

She got her degree on a sunny, humid day in June at the end of her third year. While the other students headed off to elaborate graduation parties, Anna happily went out to dinner with Sarah and ordered a Shirley Temple. She had applied to the UMASS program but was still waiting to hear, the anxiety mounting the longer she had to wait, but her aunt talked her through it, giving her whatever advice she could think of.

When her acceptance finally came in, Sarah threw her a small party, inviting their elderly neighbors and some of the neighborhood kids over for cake. Even though they had three months before she had to make the six hour trek to Massachusetts, her aunt immediately took her shopping for everything she could possibly want for her dorm room including a huge picture frame with different sized openings which they filled together with memories of Anna's time with Sarah. Then they worked to fill the summer with as many museum trips, beach days, and fancy dinners as they could. When there was only one week left before move in day, Sarah took Anna into the attic and pulled out a large gray linen box and sat her down in a dusty old wing chair.

Inside the box was a pile of photographs and a bundle of letters tied with twine. There were silk scarves, neatly folded and tucked under a small jewelry box. Sarah pulled out the photos first and handed them to Anna.

"Those are the few I was able to salvage after the funeral." Anna looked up at her aunt, surprised. "I snuck into your mother's room. I knew where she kept everything that meant the most to her." The top photo was of Teresa holding an infant Anna, a broad smile on her face as she looked right into the camera as if it was the first day of her life. "She couldn't have been happier than she was the day you were born.

Underneath was a photo of her parents together, arms around one another, with Anna sitting in front of them on a red tricycle. "I remember that tricycle. I took that thing everywhere with me. It drove my father crazy..." she trailed off, remembering all the times her father had flown off the handle about that tricycle. It had been a gift from her grandfather, her mother's father who passed away shortly after he had given it to her, and by the time she was five years old her father was convinced that she was too old for a tricycle. Every time she left it outside he would take it and put out on the curb for the trash men to pick up, and every time she would spot it and drag it back up the driveway. Finally her father got wise and waited for trash day, then handed the tricycle to the trash man and watched as he tossed it into the truck's giant metal jaws. "Dad hated that tricycle," she said quietly, tears welling in her eyes.

Sarah put her arm around Anna and leaned her cheek against her niece's forehead. "Honey, he didn't hate the tricycle, or even you for that matter. He hated himself, and he hated what he knew he had passed on to you."

"I know." Anna had spent enough time in therapy to understand that how her father had treated her was not her fault at all, but that didn't take away the sting. She sniffed and willed her eyes to dry as she flipped to the next photograph in the pile. It was a candid shot of her mother as a teenager wearing a smart gray dress and low heels, her hair in a French twist and a patent leather purse tucked under her arm.

"I took that photo of her." Sarah ran her fingers over Teresa's face, stopping at her half smile. "She was standing in the front yard of the house we grew up in back in Albany and she had just gotten her acceptance to Mount Holyoke. We were on our way out to celebrate when I snuck up on her with my camera."

"She was beautiful."

"Yes she was. And you take after her." Sarah took the photos from her and set them aside, then reached for the jewelry box. Inside was a tangle of jewelry but Sarah knew exactly what she was looking for: a silver art deco style diamond ring with little leaves engraved into the sides. "This was your mother's."

"I thought her engagement ring was yellow gold?"

"The one your father gave her was, but your mother was engaged once before she met Malcolm."

Anna felt her mind stop and her mouth fall open. She had never heard anything about another engagement. "Who was he?"

"He was a boy we went to high school with. They met when your mother was a freshman, he was a junior. He went away to architecture school and she would take the train in to visit him. Then when she decided to go off to Mount Holyoke he asked her to marry him."

"What happened?"

Sarah sighed and turned the ring over in her hand. "He died. A car accident about a month before the wedding. Your mother was devastated. Then, two years later, she met Malcolm and they got engaged almost immediately."

Anna wondered why she had never heard of this other man, her mother's first real love, and of course it was Malcolm's doing.

He forbid Teresa from thinking about Conrad Britton, her highschool sweetheart, and he made her destroy every photo of them together. He told his new wife that it was the respectful thing to do; she couldn't expect him to live with the memory of another man. In truth he just hated the idea of having been her mother's second choice. If Malcolm couldn't be first at something, he would simply erase the competition.

"Your mother hid her engagement ring under the lining of her jewelry box. She couldn't bear to part with it and once you were born she told me she wanted to be able to pass it on to you one day."

Sarah handed the ring to Anna and she slid it onto her ring finger; it fit perfectly. It was a beautiful ring that sparkled like the sun as she turned her hand from side to side, admiring its shine. "I'm glad she saved it. It's beautiful."

"Her class ring is in here somewhere too," Sarah said, rummaging through the piles of jewelry. "It's the only other thing in here I know she saved just for you. Everything else came from your father. He never understood that she didn't really care for flashy gold jewelry." She held up a gaudy diamond tennis bracelet. "Yet every birthday, Christmas, and anniversary he presented your mother with a box from the jeweler and she would pretend to be thrilled with it. She would have him help her put it on so she could wear it for a few weeks before making excuses to your father about why she had taken it off." Shaking her head, Sarah dropped the bracelet back into the box and pulled out a rose gold class ring with an amber stone, then snapped the box shut.

This was more of her mother than Anna had ever learned when she was alive and now she was sorry she hadn't taken the time to ask her mother what life had been like before meeting her father. Of course children never imagine there will come a day when their parents won't be around to answer those questions. Anna thought she had all the time in the world, that she would have her mother until she was old and gray. Now that she was older she understood that her disease had made it difficult for her to connect to her parents, her father's disease compounding the problem. She had been prickly and moody which often made her push her mother away in times when she needed her most, but now she was grateful that her aunt was giving this gift to her.

By the time they were done rummaging through the box, Anna had her hands full of photos, jewelry, and scarves that had belonged to her mother. The last thing Sarah gave her was the stack of letters, ones her mother had gotten from her high school sweetheart. "Read these someday when you need to feel something bright and lovely."

Chapter 20

With everything they had bought loaded into the bed of a borrowed pickup truck, Sarah got on the New York Thruway heading east to Massachusetts, Anna in the front seat with her feet up on the dash, staring at the map of the UMASS campus.

"Honey, you've been staring at that map for almost an hour. Are you trying to memorize it?"

"The campus is huge." Anna flipped the map sideways and pointed at her building. "I just know I'm going to get lost."

"I'm betting everyone gets lost when they get there. And I'm also betting there are plenty of upperclassmen you can ask who will point you in the right direction."

Anna shrugged and turned the map around again and frowned until her aunt snatched it away from her and threw it on the floor. "Enough of the map!" she yelled, dissolving into giggles. Laughing with her, Anna leaned her head back and closed her eyes.

"Are you sure I'm ready for this?"

Her aunt nodded, her laughter dying down. "Of course you are. You've done so much already, this is just another leg of the trip. As long as you keep taking your medication everything will be fine and no one will ever know what you've gone through." She had known that was Anna's biggest concern, that someone would find out about her diagnosis, someone other than the campus health center of course, but thankfully those records were confidential. Sarah had set Anna up with a therapist nearby in Hadley, close enough to take the bus, and she had an extra bottle of medication for the health center to hold for emergencies.

Sarah knew her niece was capable of doing the school work but she worried that she would let herself get overwhelmed by the rest of the experience. She had explained to Anna that the lecture halls would hold hundreds of students and she wasn't required to socialize with any of them. They had fought for her to have a private room in on-campus graduate housing, a luxury that was difficult to come by, but in the end Sarah had used Anna's mental illness to convince the resident advisors that it was what was best for her niece.

When she kissed Anna goodbye, Sarah turned and hurried back to the truck so that her niece wouldn't see the tears in her eyes. She loved Anna as if she was her own child and she dreaded the idea of going home to an empty house, but she was also incredibly proud of her for overcoming so much and finding herself here in graduate school, studying to become a nurse. Her illness would give her a unique insight into her patients and Sarah couldn't wait to see what Anna accomplished.

As the pickup pulled away, Anna turned away too, not wanting her aunt to see the tears flowing freely down her cheeks. She felt silly, the only adult student crying like a child as her mommy drove away on the first day of school; if she still had her mother maybe it would be a different story, but she tried not to think in "what ifs". Instead she wound her way across campus and found her building on the first try, taking the elevator to the top floor where her private room was tucked into a far corner at the end of the hall.

And in truth it was the end of her first year of graduate school when her advisor, Professor Hobart had asked to see her. She sat across from her advisor while her vision blurred, her tongue dry as sandpaper stuck to the roof of her mouth. There was a roaring in her ears that made it difficult to focus on what Hobart was saying.

"Ms. Gilman," she said, snapping her fingers in front of Anna's face. "Ms. Gilman, please."

Anna dragged her eyes up and pretended eye contact, sticking her fingers in her ears to make them pop.

Professor Hobart sighed loudly and pointedly, pulling off her glasses and tapping the edge of the lens on her desk. "Anna, your professors have reported that you've missed more classes than you've attended. You haven't turned in an assignment in weeks and the few exams you've been present for, you've managed to fail spectacularly." She pushed a piece of paper across to Anna and pointed.

But Anna didn't bother to look. She knew she had barely even written her name on the last three exams, let alone answered any of the questions. The roaring in her ears had been so loud she hadn't been able to concentrate; she had half-scribbled her name then dropped her pen on top of her exam before bolting from the room.

She knew it was her own fault for not listening to her aunt. A few months into the semester she had settled into graduate school better than she could have expected. She even managed to socialize comfortably with her peers, though just enough to say hello and ask after their studies but it was still an achievement. Her GPA held steady at nearly a 4.0 and her professors had nothing but positive feedback for her work. She was so satisfied with her success that she did exactly what she had been told not to do: she stopped taking her medication.

Nothing had changed at first, she hadn't felt any different, but then one morning she woke to a rushing noise in her head like waves crashing against the walls of her skull. She didn't know it then but she was on her way to a manic upswing and the roaring in her ears was a sign that she wouldn't be able to sleep for days to come, nor would she able to pay attention in class. Instead her mind would reel with ideas for get rich quick schemes and she would convince herself that she needed seven copies of *House of the Seven Gables* from the book store.

Then came the crash into deep depression when she stopped getting out of bed to attend classes, stopped turning in assignments, and ignored the knocks on her door from concerned classmates who had noticed her absence. Now here she was, on the verge of another upswing, sitting in front of her advisor, knowing what she was about to hear.

"Anna, I'm sorry." Folding her hands, Professor Hobart tried to look concerned but a voice in the back of Anna's head whispered *fake*. "We're going to have to dismiss you from school."

Somewhere inside her she knew she should nod, should acknowledge that she had heard and understood what Hobart was saying but she couldn't bring herself to do it. She didn't seem to have control of the part of her brain that would make her head move. As she sat in front of her advisor she could feel her eyes starting to get heavy and her jaw sagging open, she thought she might have even started to drool a little. Hobart kept talking, something about Anna not being ready for the program, needing more time to adjust, blah, blah, blah. Anna let herself stand and walk out of the office, feeling as if she was outside and three paces behind her body.

Anna barely remembered stumbling across campus in the direction of her building, fumbling to fit her key in the lock, weaving up and down the halls because she suddenly couldn't remember where her room was. As she drifted past open doors that looked in on rooms full of normal people, she noticed that most of them had started to stare. As she stared back, their normal, boring faces that all looked the same suddenly twisted and contorted, turning colors. The people who walked by her in the hallway made strange noises with their yawning mouths, the walls closing in on her as she felt a fist clamp onto her lungs.

Her dorm mates pointed and laughed at her as she turned and fled, trying to figure out how to get out of the building, screaming as she ran. The last thing she remembered was bolting down the sidewalk and out into the main road outside the campus gates where she stood on the yellow line and watched as cars rushed at her from both sides down Route 9. For the second time in her life she watched the possibility of death coming at her and all she could think about was silencing the noise in her head.

Professor Hobart was the one to call her aunt for permission to have her committed to Westborough. She helped pack up Anna's dorm room and sat with her in the lobby, waiting for Sarah to pick her up, Anna clutching the pillow she had grabbed off her bed at the last minute; Professor Hobart had done a good job of pretending not to notice.

The woman talked nonstop from the moment they stopped packing, giving Anna as many personal details as she could, though Anna couldn't understand why. It wasn't as if they were going to be friends, or trade phone numbers, but still she chattered on. She said her first name was Christine, and she went on and on about her husband and children; such an obvious way to cover up for being so blatantly nervous. Anna could tell from her unending stream of nonsense that she didn't want to be stuck sitting there with a crazy person.

When Sarah finally pulled up in front of the dorm building Professor Hobart shook her hand as if it was parents weekend, introducing herself with a plastic smile glued to her face, but then she turned to Anna and said with genuine warmth, "You're going to be just fine Miss Gilman."

After a number of failed attempts at starting a conversation, Sarah and Anna lapsed into stony silence and drove the entire hour and a half without saying a word. The moment her aunt's car came to a stop in front of the main entrance, an orderly jogged down the stairs and opened Anna's door while a severe-looking blond woman in a suit stood at the top of the stairs, waiting. The rushing sound in her ears mounted to a fever pitch and she couldn't hear a word her aunt was saying. Anna lagged and Sarah reached out for her elbow, just like she had at her mother's funeral, and helped her up the stairs, the orderly hovering a few steps behind just in case Anna decided to make a run for it. She looked down as she moved, studiously put one foot in front of the other, trying not to stumble and fall in front of these strangers. When she looked up again, the blond nurse was still standing there but she no longer had a face; instead there was an open, black hole where her face should have been and her jaw hinged open like a snake's. Frowning, Anna continued past her through the front doors, her aunt's hand never leaving her arm.

Her vision was unfocused and blurred but she could make out the cracked marble floor, the peeling main staircase that had seen better days. But as she looked around blankly, she somehow knew she had landed somewhere important and perhaps these people could make the voices go away. She and Sarah followed the blond down a hallway that could have been three feet long or three miles for all Anna knew, and led them into a cramped little office.

"My name is Valerie Martin. I'm the nursing supervisor on this ward." The woman held out her hand and it wobbled like a goldfish as Anna stared at it, wondering if it would feel like a fish too and a tiny giggle escaped her lips as Valerie's hand circled her reed-thin fingers. "Dr. Brown will be your attending psychiatrist, you'll see him later today when he's done meeting with some of our new hires." She looked down at the suitcase in Anna's hand and pointed. "You can put that down by the door."

Valerie cleared a stack of files off of a chair covered in a sickly shade of green corduroy, then did the same with a giant yellow plastic one that was shaped like a fan. She motioned for both Anna and Sarah to take a seat. Anna perched on the edge of the green chair, watching Valerie as she settled herself into her own red leather chair behind her giant metal desk. Sarah sank into the ugly green chair, a puff of dust escaping from the cushion.

As Anna looked around she noticed there was very little in the office that made it Valerie's; no photographs, no cork boards with greeting cards pinned to it. Maybe this woman was just as desperate and disconnected as Anna was, or maybe she just didn't like bringing her personal life to work. Anna shrugged as she played out a conversation in her head, jumping like a startled cat when Valerie spoke again.

"So, Anna. Tell me about yourself."

A loaded question. Did she want to know about Anna, the straight A student who didn't have a care in the world until her mother died? Or did she want to know about the Anna who got kicked out of school because she couldn't get out of bed to go to classes?

"I'm originally from Buffalo. Both my parents are dead."

"Anna's mother was killed a number of years ago," Sarah interjected. "And her father died a few years after that. She's been living with me since my sister passed."

Valerie nodded and opened a folder in front of her, a fresh blue intake form on top. "Good to know. Let's rewind a bit and start with some basic questions." She turned back to Anna. "Is that ok?"

Anna shrugged and nodded blankly, twisting an errant piece of hair that had slipped out of her messy ponytail. She answered all the easy questions: her birthday, her parents' names, whether or not she had ever broken a bone.

"Do you feel sad most days?"

"I guess," Anna whispered, watching as Valerie checked a box.

"Do you hear voices?" Valerie was careful not to look up, not wanting to give the question too much weight, even though Anna knew this was the question that mattered.

"I don't know. I guess so." She wasn't sure if the white noise in her head counted, if the sounds people made when their faces twisted could be considered voices. Valerie expertly hid her reaction as she checked another box. Valerie knew she meant to say yes.

"And do you see things that aren't there?"

Cocking her head to the side like a dog listening for a whistle, Anna chewed her lip and considered Valerie's question. "Sometimes faces look twisted, like they're melting, and the walls tilt. Does that count?"

Valerie checked a box and nodded. "We'll count that as a yes, just in case."

Anna's eyes wandered to the bookshelves that lined the walls of the office. The middle shelves held the usual old psychology texts, the latest iteration of the DSM, and a few other books about nursing and behavior. The top shelf though held a number of slimmer volumes. Valerie caught her looking and waved her hand at the books. "Those are my journals. I've kept one since the day I started on the wards of Northampton State Hospital in 1959."

"Why?"

"Writing is therapeutic." Valerie shrugged. "I also didn't want to forget any of my patients. Or any of my experiences."

Even Anna's fuzzy head could recognize that was a reasonable concept, though she had a hard time understanding why you would want to write down every experience, good or bad but some people were like that.

"Anna prefers to read, rather than write," Sarah said, smiling like she was on some kind of game show. Anna turned her attention back to Valerie and chewed her lip while Valerie jotted down a few notes.

"Now Sarah…" Valerie turned her attention to Anna's aunt, her guardian she supposed, the one who would give her consent for Anna to be committed, and asked all kinds of medical questions. Sarah dug out her insurance card and listed off the names of all of Anna's doctors, then signed what seemed like a hundred forms while Anna's mind wandered in and out, a haze clouding her mind.

"Alright," Valerie said, closing the folder. "That's the paperwork. How about I show you to your room?"

Sarah stood and gathered Anna in a tight hug, her shoulders vibrating with muffled sobs, then pushed Anna away, nearly shoving her into Valerie and ran from the room with her hand over her mouth. Valerie caught Anna's arm and ushered her out into the hallway and up the stairs to the second floor where they hung a left then their first right into a tiny room with a narrow wrought iron bed that was white but most of the paint had chipped away; a thin blue and white striped mattress was rolled up at the head of the bed with a pillow stacked on top. An orderly came in and unrolled the mattress, then handed Anna a set of sheets, a gray wool blanket, and a plaid wool throw, then excused himself to leave her alone with Valerie who had grabbed Anna's suitcase on their way out of her office.

Anna moved slowly over to the closet and dropped her case on the floor with a thud that echoed in her head. Turning to look out the window, Anna realized she could see all the way down to the lake and she was momentarily blinded by the sun glinting off of the water's surface. She closed her eyes and watched the ghosts of the sun's rays bob behind her lids.

"It's a beautiful view of the lake, isn't it?"

Anna felt herself smile for the first time in months. "It's so peaceful."

"Piece of advice Miss Gilman, don't settle in here." Valerie turned and left Anna to unpack, hanging her clothes in the tiny closet, pulling her books out of the bottom of her case and stacking them next to her bed. She reached out slowly to put the sheets and blanket on the naked mattress then tucked her pillow under the blanket so it wouldn't collect dust. Shortly after she settled in there was a knock at the door and an orderly came in pushing a metal cart stacked with charts and loaded down with bubble packs filled with rainbow-colored pills.

"Hello Anna. My name is Alice. I work the evening shift on this ward." She held out a trio of tiny pills and a paper cup filled with water.

"Oh I don't take medication."

The nurse smiled sweetly, then pushed the pills into the palm of Anna's hand. "It's your first night here. You're going to want to get some sleep honey."

Anna stared at the pills and watched as they started to wiggle in her hand. Maybe the nurse was right-- she needed some sleep. Popping them in her mouth, Anna took a gulp of water and washed down the pills, then showed Nurse Alice her empty mouth.

That night, after lights out Anna lay in her bed and listened to the sounds of the ward preparing for sleep, surprised at how loud it was. Even after all the other patients had settled in there was still noise. The shuffle of the nurses and orderlies doing room checks, the phones ringing at all hours while computers hummed and beeped in the background. She waited for the medication to kick in, to knock her out and drown the noises, but sleep wouldn't come. Well into the night she lay like that, on her back, her eyes fixed to the ceiling. Most of the nurses had gone off shift and the orderlies were playing cards in the break room. As quiet as it had gotten, the building itself made noise all through the night and into the morning hours.

By morning Anna felt groggy and disoriented, exhausted from lack of sleep and the shock of everything that had happened the day before. She lay in bed, flexing her fingers and toes, trying to get rid of the pins and needles. Laying in the same position for nine hours had done her tired body no favors, she thought as she tried to sit up and swing her legs over the edge of her bed. She put her feet flat on the hardwood floor and wondered, for no reason at all, if those were the original floors from the 1860's. It didn't matter, scars were scars no matter how old.

That morning she ventured out onto the wards, heading for the day room where some of the patients were milling around before breakfast. Anna eyed them all warily but of course none of them looked at her. It wasn't like the first day of school where everyone was trying to decide which clique to join. This was an insane asylum where no one wanted to connect, just in case that person happened to be even crazier than they were. She waited close to the door, waiting for someone to guide them down to the cafeteria where she would find herself surrounded by even more patients and the unidentifiable smells of unrecognizable food items.

Following the others' lead, Anna took a brown plastic tray and reached under the plexiglass sneeze guard for a lukewarm plate of what looked like scrambled eggs and soggy toast spread with butter substitute that gave the bread a vaguely orange tinge. Tea and coffee were served in cream colored plastic tureens which were better suited to chicken noodle soup but instead were filled with decaffeinated swill with packets of fake sugar and powdered creamer on the side. She sat down at a table near the window and stared out as her food congealed on her plate and her tea went stone cold. As she glanced out across the courtyard, she thought she saw a curtain move in one of the windows.

Chapter 21

Anna Gilman had been a patient at Westborough for two years and according to her file she had shown no progress; in fact, as of late, it had been noted repeatedly that she had regressed in her delusions, imagining that she was there for some kind of internship and that she had made friends with her psychiatrist, a young intern who had graduated top of her class at Wesleyan and was just finishing up medical school at Harvard.

In spite of the reintroduction of her medication, Anna found that the sounds and visions had not subsided; if anything they had gotten worse and she had become fixated on that one room in the old ward. When she was finally forced to face what was happening in her mind, Anna realized it wasn't Peder who had been wandering off in the night, it was she who had been sleep walking. Nearly every night since her arrival at Westborough Anna had taken herself to that room and she had stayed there until whichever nurse was doing bed checks discovered her room empty and came looking for her. As the nurses led her back to her room, she regaled them with tales of seeing her mother who had spoken to her in that room.

When she was finally taken to see Dr. Brown, Anna's mind had betrayed her completely and she had no idea what was real and what wasn't. All she knew was that she had been committed by her aunt, her poor aunt who had done everything she could to keep this from happening, this very thing. Sarah had tried her best to keep Anna from unraveling but in the end she had simply delayed the inevitable.

"Dr. Westcott tells me you've been having some vivid hallucinations." Dr. Brown sat across from her, not on the other side of his desk but in a chair that was angled kitty corner to hers so that there was no barrier between them. His face, though red and paunchy, was open and not at all unkind. "Tell me about that."

"There's not much to say. I keep seeing my mother and she keeps saying that there are roses but I don't know what any of it means."

"How much do you remember about your mother's death?"

Anna closed her eyes and took a deep breath, then told Dr. Brown what she could recall: dinner, her father, the argument about the duck, her shoes. Then she got to the part where she stormed out of the restaurant and wandered the streets until a policeman found her. "When we got back to the hotel there were policemen everywhere. The one who brought me back told me that something terrible had happened to my mother but my father, he was so angry at me that he wouldn't even let the cop tell me what had happened. He threw him out."

"He threw him out?"

Anna nodded. "He told him that he would deal with me, and I thought he was going to yell at me for leaving the restaurant by myself but instead he blew up at me. He started saying that my mother was dead and it was all my fault." Tears began to roll down her cheeks; Dr. Brown handed her a tissue and waited for her to get herself together. "I finally found out that she had been murdered. It was weeks later and I overheard him talking to my Aunt Sarah, my mother's sister."

Brown nodded and jotted down a few quick notes, then turned his attention back to Anna. "And what did you hear them say?"

"My father said that after I left the restaurant, my mother yelled at him for upsetting me. She understood that there was something not right inside me, and that I was starting to have mood swings like my father's."

"Was your father ever violent with either one of you?"

Shaking her head, Anna stuck her thumb in her mouth and chewed on her nail. "No, not physically anyway. He was just...explosive. His temper was unpredictable, we never knew what would set him off or how long he would stay angry. Sometimes it was the smallest things, things that would never make a normal person angry like when my mother would buy white American cheese instead of yellow. It would set him off and he would scream at her, call her all kinds of names."

"And he was like that with you as well?"

"Yes. He hated everything about me, everything I did and said. He told my mother on multiple occasions that their marriage was ruined when I came along. He hated sharing my mother's attention and it just reinforced his feelings when he realized I had the same problems he did."

Brown watched her over the rims of his glasses, scratching the side of his nose with his pen. "Tell me more about your mother's passing."

"Well, I heard my father say that she had yelled at him then stormed off, presumably to go look for me." She looked down at her hands, then up at Brown, his eyes glued to her as if she was the most interesting patient he had ever had. "While I was wandering the streets my mother was stabbed to death by a strange man on a strange sidewalk in Canada. And my father blamed for it."

"Anna," Brown said, sitting forward and reaching out to pat the back of her hand. "Your mother's death wasn't your fault at all, not in the least."

"Logically," she said, "of course I know that. But then I stop taking my medication and on those downswings all I can think is, my God he's right. If I hadn't thrown a fit and left the restaurant she never would have been on that sidewalk and she'd still be alive." Anna stared off into the middle distance above the doctor's head and took a deep breath. "And then I keep thinking and I think, if I wasn't sick I wouldn't have thrown that fit. If I wasn't born at all, I wouldn't be sick."

"Cyclical thinking. It's a vicious circle." Chuckling, Brown leaned back and shook his head. "Your illness is not your fault. Bipolar is a vicious disease that doesn't want to be controlled. It wants to control you." He stood and stretched his legs, then held out his hand to Anna. "Now, if you want to get your life back, we need to keep talking and work through what you feel about your mother's death. But for the moment, our time is up. I'm not going to change your medications just yet."

Taking his hand, Anna stood and felt him squeeze her fingers warmly. "Thank you Dr. Brown. She could feel the liquid sedative spreading through her veins, making her eyes heavy and her brain foggy. Brown must have noticed the effects since they hadn't been talking more than twenty minutes. He understood; he seemed to be far nicer than the nurses gave him credit for. There was an orderly waiting for her in the hall-- not one of the ones who had escorted her here- and he led her back to her room where Harper was waiting for her.

"How was your talk with Brown?" she asked without preamble.

Sighing, Anna let Harper into her room and pulled the chair out from her desk. "It was fine. It didn't last long because the sedative is kicking in but he asked me about my mother."

Harper nodded, looking serious. "I figured as much. He has my notes so he knows what ground we've covered together. You do understand that's what happens between us right? Patient and therapist?"

"Yes," Anna replied, exhausted by all these newfound revelations. "I'm sorry for the way I spoke to you. I wasn't in my right mind."

"I know," Harper said, reaching out and squeezing her arm. "That's why you're here, so we can get you back in your right mind and hopefully keep you there."

Harper was her therapist. She understood that now as she looked at this young woman who could have been her classmate, maybe even her friend. They might have passed notes in class or studied together, maybe even gone to the movies or out on double dates. Instead Harper was sitting at Anna's bedside, watching her like a hawk because she was losing her mind and had no idea who or what she was.

"I'm glad you were able to talk to him. I hope he's able to help you remember more about that night." The sigh Harper let out encompassed so much more than just the frustration of a stalled process. She was truly concerned about Anna. "Listen, I really am your friend, not in the traditional sleepover party way but in the sense that I have really enjoyed getting to know you and talking with you."

"Same here," she agreed. "I appreciate everything you've done for me, but it was stupid of me to think the medication would fix everything. Not after a massive break like what I had at graduate school." It was going to take far more than medication to put her pieces back together.

"We'll figure it out Anna, I promise." Harper picked up the book about the Fox sisters, the one Anna had checked out of the library. "I can't imagine reading this trash is helping any," she said, waving the book at her. "You know they admitted that they were lying right?"

Anna hadn't known that, but even if she had, she still would have read the book and she still would have wondered if it was all possible, talking to the dead. It wasn't so much a belief in ghosts, but a need to believe that her mother was still out there somewhere, still a part of her. Even if the Fox sisters were fakes, even if the entire concept of Spiritualism was just one giant hoax, Anna still hoped her mother could see her, maybe even come to her in her dreams. But she also knew that was a slippery slope, seeing her mother; it was such a fine line between dream and hallucination, a line that Anna's mind couldn't possibly discern.

As she watched Harper walk out of her room, Anna picked up the book and tossed it back on the pile, then climbed into bed. It was time to sleep off the sedative and start again in a few hours when it had worn off. As she slept, she dreamed about that night, the night her mother died. She corrected herself-- murdered. Even in her dreams she couldn't bring herself to say it but that was the plain truth. Her mother had been stabbed to death on a city street in a foreign country while searching the night for her mentally ill daughter. No matter what the doctors or therapists told her she couldn't stop herself from laying the blame squarely at her feet. They had never caught him, the man who brutally relieved her mother of her last breath, so there was no one else to point the finger at.

By the time the police stumbled on her mother's body, the killer was long gone. The best they could make out from the angle of the blows was that it was a man and that he had startled her, causing her to turn and stumble, catching the knife first in her abdomen, then in the heart. The other stab wounds were just for show as she was already dead. Then he left her on the sidewalk, blood pooling beneath her, her eyes still wide open in shock, staring up at the night sky. All the while Anna had been wandering the streets, angry at her father, secretly wishing he was dead, not knowing that instead it would be her mother who would be taken away.

Sometimes she wondered about the man who had killed her mother. Had Teresa been his intended target? Had he spotted her coming out of the restaurant and followed her? The police surmised it had been a robbery gone wrong-- wrong place at the wrong time kind of thing- but nothing had been taken. One officer remarked callously that perhaps Mrs. Gilman had simply been an easy target and considering the number of tourists that crossed the borders every day, the chances of them ever solving the case were nearly zero. They said it was probably some transient, someone with some sort of mental illness that drove him to kill.

Of course Anna understood that being mentally ill could make you do things you wouldn't typically do, but she always wondered what had to snap inside of you to lead you to take the life of another human being. It was one thing to think it, as she had with her father, to feel the hatred for another person well up inside you and imagine what it would be like if that person was gone, but this man hadn't even known her mother. She had never done anything to him that would have provoked such a brutal attack. This was a dangerous train of thought for Anna; it always led to the question of whether or not she herself was capable of something like murder. Even in her most manic phases she had never been aggressive and on her downswings she only ever harmed herself.

Was the man who murdered her mother handsome? Was he intelligent? Did he have a job? Regardless of what the police thought, Anna imagined that he held a steady job, maybe even had a family, and killing her mother had been a fluke, something he had been driven to do out of some level of inner desperation that he couldn't explain, not even to his wife who had no idea where he went for hours on end every day. Over the years Anna had built up this bizarre fantasy version of the murderer as a deeply depressed individual who liked to spend hours sitting in the park, just indulging in the darkness that clouded his mind, much like Anna, but his darkness had taken a different, more dangerous turn the night he decided to take a knife with him.

In the daylight hours Anna knew that her image of this killer was far from reality, that the police were probably right and that the man was a transient, maybe even homeless, just passing through. Her mother was indeed in the wrong place at the wrong time, and that was the thought she woke with in the middle of the night when the sedative had finally found its way out of her system. An asylum ward at night was a strange thing. You knew it was night because it was dark outside, but still there was a glow of light that never went away no matter how late it was. There was the pool of fluorescence given off by the nurses' station, the soft flickering of the safety lights high up where the wall met the ceiling.

Like a regular hospital the noise too was constant. There was always the sound of muffled voices and floors creaking under careful footsteps. The fax machine droned through the night and the computers hummed around the clock. There were nurses doing checks, orderlies dispensing meds that had to be given day and night. It was a city that never slept, yet there was never anything to do in the middle of the night but lay there and think, so that was what Anna did. She thought about her aunt, her massive failure in school. Then she thought about Peder, how he looked at her, how he talked to her, how he had kissed her. She also thought about how violent and terrifying he could be, the mood swings that were so violent they put hers to shame.

Peder had mentioned once that he often did things without remembering them, like the trances he had fallen into when he was young, wandering out into the fields behind his house. Schizophrenia was a dangerous illness, far more dangerous than Bipolar, and Anna sometimes wondered if Peder was capable of hurting someone. On the other hand, she also found herself wondering if he was capable of great love. There had been something in his kiss that told her he was, but that too was dangerous; great love often led to great disappointment. Peder didn't strike her as the type of man who could handle a great disappointment, especially when it came to romance.

After hours of laying there like that, thinking about things that she shouldn't have been, Anna finally saw the first hints of dawn slipping through the cracks where the shades didn't quite meet the sill. Getting out of bed she wrapped herself in her robe and shuffled out into the day room and tucked herself into one of the sofas, propping her chin in her hand as she stared out into the distance, not seeing much of anything clearly. A hand on her shoulder startled her out of her fog and she looked up to find Peder standing behind the couch.

"You look a little rough around the edges." He came around and sat next to Anna elbowing her playfully in the ribs. "How are you doing slugger?"

Shrugging, Anna held her hand out and wobbled it side to side. "So-so. I mean, I've been better."

"Things could be worse though, right? You could be in isolation somewhere in the bowels of this place."

"Good point," she replied, smiling slightly. "How about you? How have you been passing the days since my impromptu incarceration?"

"I've been worried in all honesty."

"About me?"

Peder nodded and reached out to touch her knee, her legs folded under her at an angle facing him, and let his fingertips linger on her thigh. "Yes. I was worried about you. How could I not be?"

"Look where we are," Anna laughed coldly. "We're in an insane asylum. All there is to do here is worry, why would I assume you would worry about me in particular?"

Eyeing her for a moment, Peder squeezed her thigh warmly and patted her leg, somehow frowning and smiling at the same time. "Because we're connected Anna. I've told you that many times before."

And each time he said it, something inside her balked, yet she had let him kiss her; here she was, his hand on her leg, and she did nothing about it. Instead she reveled in the warmth that his fingers impressed upon her skin. "You say that, but how do you know?"

"I just do." He looked down at the floor but didn't take his hand from her leg as she reached out and covered his strong fingers with her own in a sort of gesture of acquiescence even though there were still a thousand alarm bells with red flashing lights blaring in the back of her mind.

"How can we be connected when I don't even feel connected to myself?"

"That's just how it is in places like these." Leaning back, he stretched both arms across the back of the sofa, letting his hand drop casually to Anna's shoulder. "All you have to do is let me in and then you'll find it a lot easier to get to know yourself. I promise."

His words made her feel safe, comforted in a way she hadn't in quite some time, not since her last stable period so many years ago under the watchful eye of her aunt. All she really wanted was to feel as if someone was there to keep her from disintegrating into nothingness and the look in Peder's eye gave her a spark of hope, the tiniest shred of expectation.

"I'll try, that's the best I can do."

Peder smiled broadly and tapped Anna's shoulder. "That's all I ask." He stood and strode out of the day room leaving Anna alone.

"Miss Gilman?" She jumped a mile as Alice Lambert snuck up on her. "Sorry, didn't mean to scare you. Miss Martin is on her way up for you."

"Oh ok." Alice continued to stare at Anna though Anna had no idea why. "Thank you?"

"Well, perhaps you might want to get dressed?"

Anna looked down, realizing she was still in her robe, and stood. "Yes, I suppose I should. Thank you."

She took her time getting back to her room, then dressed carefully and straightened up her room while she waited for Valerie to come for her. She wondered what the woman wanted since she so very rarely checked in, despite what she had said to Anna the day she condemned her to Dr. Brown.

There was a curt knock on the door and Valerie strode in, reaching out to shake Anna's hand as if they were meeting for the first time. "You look much better Anna. How are you feeling?" Without being asked, Valerie pulled up a chair and motioned for Anna to take the bed.

"I'm feeling much better thank you."

"And how are your sessions with Dr. Brown?"

Anna shrugged halfheartedly. "They're fine."

Valerie looked doubtful but she smiled anyway and patted the back of Anna's hand, the touch worlds away from Peder's. "So the reason I came up here is that I'm concerned."

"More than usual?" Anna asked with more sarcasm than she had intended.

"Yes, actually," Valerie replied rather coldly, obviously miffed at Anna's tone. "I was told you were sitting with Mr. Roderick this morning and the two of you were rather cozy."

"We were talking this morning, yes. But I don't see how that's your business."

"It's my business, Anna, because Mr. Roderick is not only dangerous but extremely manipulative." She shifted on the chair and tried to get Anna to make eye contact as she spoke, conveying the relative seriousness of what she was saying. "I've seen this kind of behavior before in paranoid schizophrenics. He's trying to win you over so that he can go on to convince you that there's nothing wrong with him. He may even try to tell you he doesn't belong in an asylum when I can tell you beyond a shadow of a doubt that he does."

As she paused to take a breath, Anna finally looked up at Valerie, her brow creased in a frown, little beads of moisture collecting on her top lip.

"Anna, do you want to get better? Maybe even leave this place someday?"

"Of course." Wasn't that the goal? To get her back on medications and eventually send her back to her aunt? "Why, is there a chance I could stay?" Anna sat up straight and slid to the edge of her mattress, gazing intently at Valerie as if the answer would suddenly appear on her forehead.

"If you aren't careful Mr. Roderick will drag you into his world and you'll never surface again. If that happens…" She trailed off and looked at Anna meaningfully but she wasn't certain what Valerie meant.

"If that happens, then what? What will happen to me?"

"You risk a total regression. Look what happened when you met him just months ago. You were right back to square one with your delusions and hallucinations. He did that. He tipped you over the edge into thinking you were something you're not. Do you want that again?"

Anna shook her head sadly. Valerie was right, things were going well until she caught sight of Peder and began imagining a world that didn't exist where she was somehow separate from someone like him when in reality here she was, locked away just as he was.

"I suggest you limit your dealings with Mr. Roderick. He's not a positive influence on you." With that she stood to go, then reached into her pocket and pulled out Anna's journal, handing it back to her. "Remember what I told you about not settling in here. If there ever was a time to reflect on that, it's now." And she left the room, her footsteps echoing down the hall and through the door to the stairwell that would take her back to her office while Anna was left, saddened, slumped on the edge of her bed.

Sometimes she thought that Peder was the one of the few who truly understood her but now, as she mulled over what Valerie said, she recognized that was all part of his game. He had charmed her like an Indian snake charmer lured the cobra from its basket. She felt the old fear return as she wondered what it was he planned to do with her now that she had poked her head out of her basket. Turning the journal over in her hands, she wondered just how much of it Valerie had read. She also wondered how many people Valerie had shared it with, but there was nothing she could do about that now. Instead she went to her desk and settled in with a pen to think out everything that had happened.

Once she put pen to paper she couldn't stop. She wrote about everything that floated into her mind-- her breakdown, the look on her aunt's face when she signed her over to the hospital's care; all things she had forced out of her consciousness for nearly two years while she languished in the throes of the grandest delusion she had ever crafted. As she wrote, she realized how grateful she was that Harper had taken such a gentle approach with her, guiding her through the course of her delusion rather than trying to force her back to a reality she wasn't ready to face just yet.

It was also time to take a good hard look at what she wanted from her time at Westborough. Now that her medication was stabilized and she was capable of a level of introspection, she wrote down a list of goals she wanted to accomplish in her remaining time, however long that may be. Then she wrote down a list of reasons to keep Peder Roderick at arm's length.

"Hard at work?" Anna turned to find Peder standing in her doorway, smiling down at her with eyebrows raised. She rushed to close her journal and tuck it away before he could see what she was writing.

"Not really. Just doodling." Dropping her pen, Anna turned and leaned her elbow over the back of her chair. "What can I do for you?"

Peder took a step into her room and looked around, taking in every inch of her space, making her feel as if her privacy was being violated somehow but she tried not to show him how uncomfortable she was. He struck her as the kind of person who could smell fear. "Nothing in particular. I just came for a quick visit. It won't take them long to realize I'm in the wrong wing," he said with a wink. Sitting on the edge of the bed, Peder patted the empty space next to him, expecting Anna to join him.

"Best if I stayed over here," she replied, shaking her head sternly. "As you said, it won't be long before they find you here."

"Ah, don't want to get into trouble I see." He shrugged and leaned back against her pillow, making himself at home. Next thing he would be kicking his feet up onto her blankets. "Understandable. Wouldn't want my reputation to taint you." Anna thought she detected a shift in his tone though his facial expression was placid. She watched him appear to be completely relaxed but she could see that his muscles were tense, ready for something; fight or flight Anna thought. She silently prayed that an orderly would come along to do room checks so that she wouldn't have to ask Peder to leave and risk setting him off.

What had she been thinking, letting him kiss her, letting him touch her? He had said she need only let him in and she had stupidly allowed him far closer than she should have. He said he knew all about her, but she realized he only knew the illusion, or the delusion as the case may be, and he was happy to help her perpetuate it.

"Have you adjusted to your medications yet?"

"Yes," she said carefully, wondering where he was headed with the question.

"Still feeling slow?" he asked casually, barely making eye contact with her, and even though she was indeed still feeling quite sluggish and foggy something told her not to admit it to him.

"Actually no, I've been feeling much more myself these days."

He regarded her out of the corner of his eye, folding his hands behind his head to add to the image of a casual conversationalist but the wheels in his head were turning. "That's good. We wouldn't want you any less than alert, now would we?"

As she considered the tone of his statement, an orderly poked his head inside and caught site of Peder laying on her bed as if he belonged there. "Mr. Roderick, we have been looking everywhere for you." The orderly took Peder roughly by the elbow and hauled him to his feet, ignoring the childish grin Peder shot him. He was pleased that the orderly was angry. "I'm sorry Miss Gilman. I hope he wasn't bothering you."

Anna was about to say something but wisely changed her mind and chose to stay quiet, instead giving the orderly a meaningful look that she hoped Peder didn't catch. The younger man nodded curtly and escorted Peder out of the room and down the hall. Anna stood and pushed her door closed, leaning heavily against it, listening to the sound of her own breathing, the hammering of her heart inside her chest, knocking as if it might burst out at any moment.

Chapter 22

It was not long after when Valerie announced that she would be retiring. Actually, it wasn't so much an announcement as a quiet spreading of the news, passed through the staff and eventually the patients. It carried with it an air of shock and surprise; most everyone assumed that Valerie would grow old, perhaps even die still working at Westborough. What could she possibly find to do with herself if she was no longer working for the Department? So far as the staff was concerned, Westborough *was* Valerie's life.

However, everyone knew for certain that it was pointless to try to make a big deal about her leaving; Valerie wasn't a cake and speeches kind of person but Anna felt a strange sort of devastation at the idea of losing Valerie and she wanted the opportunity to say goodbye, so late one afternoon she snuck past the nurses' station and down the main stairs where she cautiously sidled up to her door, only to find that Valerie was on the phone having what sounded like a rather heated discussion with someone.

"Bill, are you sure you can't find someone else for this?"

Anna pressed herself against the wall just outside the door as she heard Valerie sigh heavily.

"They must be desperate if they're willing to put off my retirement." Valerie paused, waiting for this Bill character to finish talking. "When would I have to be back in Northampton?"

She was going back? The way Valerie had always talked about Northampton State Hospital Anna assumed that chapter of her life was closed forever.

"Fine. I'll be there....I've always liked that white cottage so I guess there's something of a silver lining...yes that's fine. Noon in your office. See you then."

Valerie hung up and Anna waited a few minutes before making her presence known. "Valerie?"

Looking up, she waved Anna in and pointed to the couch. "How much of that did you hear?"

"Not much," Anna shrugged.

"So you heard everything then."

Anna blushed, caught in an unsuccessful lie. "Yes. I thought you hated Northampton."

"What would make you think that?"

Shrugging, Anna chose her words carefully. "You've not said much about your time there except the technical things like the daily running of the wards and the changes you made. It doesn't sound like you made many connections there."

"On the contrary," Valerie replied. Anna thought she saw the hint of a smile pulling at the corners of her lips. "I made many connections in that place, but given the nature of a beast like that, they weren't long lasting and they're best left in the past." She shook her head and laughed, a harsh and rather unkind laugh. "And I there I hoped they would stay but it seems that's not what the universe has in store for me."

"Why are you going back?"

Valerie lifted a shoulder and tapped her pen on her calendar which Anna now noticed was quite a bit more empty, the days to her retirement numbered in red. "They need someone to do some cataloging of files for the Department of Mental Health. They know I could do the job in my sleep so..." She held her hands palms up as if to say, *I'm their gal.* "It is what it is."

"Can I ask you something?"

"Of course."

"What will you do when you finally retire?"

Valerie laughed. "You mean, do I have anything to look forward to aside from my job?"

"No, that's not what I was thinking…"

"It's ok," she replied, leaning back in her chair and stretching her arms. "I know it's what everyone is thinking. To be honest I don't know. All I know is that I want a small home of my own, preferably nowhere near a hospital, with a garden and a library. Maybe some place to write. Who knows? Maybe one day I'll write my memoirs. Or maybe I'll just waste my days away reading about lives far more interesting than my own."

"Your life is very interested," Anna argued. "You've dedicated so many years to helping other people. Doesn't that count?"

"Of course it does." Anna watched as Valerie looked around her office, taking in her sparse surroundings, her office that looked barely used aside from the piles of folders. "I suppose I never really let myself get used to being here, but then isn't that what I warned you against? It's never a good idea to get complacent in your surroundings. That's how you get hurt." Just as suddenly as she had opened up, Valerie's expression suddenly slammed shut and she was all business again. "You obviously didn't come down here to talk about me and it's getting late. What can I do for you?"

"Well, I...I just wanted to say goodbye really."

"I appreciate that Miss Gilman." Anna watched as Valerie's face softened, moisture collecting on her bottom lashes. "I've enjoyed my time here at Westborough and I've enjoyed meeting you, meeting all of the patients here. But I believe you are in good hands with Dr. Brown and Dr. Westcott. I know that in time you will write to me or call me to tell me that you are out and making a success of your life in one way or another."

"Thank you for having such confidence in me."

"It has nothing to do with confidence," Valerie replied shaking her head. She raised her finger and pointed it at Anna like a school mistress lecturing a pupil. "It's the natural order of things. You cannot stay here. You, of all people, are capable of getting well, of conquering this disease and going back out into the world. You'll see."

Thanking Valerie again for her kind words, Anna stood to go, but as she went to leave, she felt the overwhelming urge to hug Valerie. She rushed behind Valerie's desk and threw her arms around the woman's neck, burying her face in Valerie's hair and inhaling her clean, crisp scent. "Thank you for everything Valerie."

And with that, she ran from the room, up the stairs, and back to the ward where Nurse Lambert waited at the nurses' station with her medication.

"Here you are Miss Gilman. Did you have a good visit with Miss Martin?"

Anna took the cup and the pills, washed them down, and opened her mouth for Nurse Lambert to see. "I did, thank you." She smiled politely and headed to the day room where they were showing a movie; some Disney-esque rated G concoction that someone had dug out of the library. There were strict rules as to what the patients could and couldn't watch given their varied diagnoses. Nothing with too much violence, an abundance of romance, or anything magical, mystical, or mythological. Taking a seat in the corner, Anna pretended to watch the movie but instead sat and mulled over her conversation with Valerie. Would she ever be ready to go back out into the world and start her life over? As she glanced around at the other patients, some catatonic, others rocking gently in their seats, she realized that Valerie was right: she did have the greatest chance of moving on, but what would that mean exactly?

She looked at all the nurses and orderlies propped against the walls, watching the movie with the patients, their eyes intermittently flitting over the group and taking a silent count of all the patients; Peder was conspicuously absent but then he would be after his little stunt in Anna's room. Maybe someday she could finish her degree and come back to work in a place like this. Probably not Westborough since it would likely be closed by the time she got out and managed to finish what she had started, but there were psych wards in nearly every hospital in the nation. There were even rumors that they were going to build a whole new facility at Worcester someday that would take the place of the abandoned one that was just rotting away on that hill at the crest of Belmont Street.

Out of the corner of her eye she saw Harper sneak in and join the group, scanning the crowd for Anna until she made eye contact with her patient and smiled. Anna hoped Harper was pleased to see her out of her room and joining in a group activity, a rare occurrence for someone like her. Nodding her approval, Harper turned and disappeared. It occurred Anna as she looked up at the clock that it was the end of Harper's shift; it was nearing ten she saw with a start, far later than she realized, and she too separated herself from the group and slowly made her way back to her room.

As she rounded the corner she saw someone moving quickly down the hallway in the opposite direction. From a distance she thought it looked a lot like Peder but she had assumed he was confined to his room as punishment for being found in Anna's room. Maybe it was one of the male orderlies who, in the dark, looked like Peder from behind. Shrugging it off, Anna reached her room and went to push the door open when she saw that it was already ajar, propped open by a piece of gray wood. Kicking the wood out of the way, she tried to get in her room but the door seemed to be stuck, hitting something behind it which was strange because there was barely enough furniture in her room to furnish it, let alone block the door.

Slipping through the tiny wedge of space between the door and the jamb, Anna stopped just inside her doorway and gasped. Her room had been destroyed, everything in it ruined. Her desk was smashed to pieces, her pens and pencils strewn everywhere. Her blankets were in a heap on the floor and her mattress had been pulled from the bedframe and left standing on its end, collapsing on itself like a giant rectangular marshmallow. The little gray desk chair was in splinters and it dawned on Anna that a chunk of the chair was what had been used to prop open her door while all her books were torn to pieces and piled behind the door. She rushed over to what remained of her desk and realized that in all the carnage thrown about her room, the one thing she didn't see was her journal.

Frantic, she ran out into the hallway and began to yell as tears streamed down her face. A crowd of orderlies and nurses came running, two of them reaching out and grabbing her by the elbows as if to restrain her. "No, no," she sobbed. "My room. Look in my room."

Nurse Lambert had already gingerly stepped through the doorway and was surveying the damage. She toed aside the decimated books and took in the chunks of busted wood, the wrecked bed, and the contents of Anna's closet spilling onto the floor.

"My god," she muttered. "Who would have done this?"

Anna sobbed and reached for Nurse Lambert's hand. "My journal is gone Alice. Whoever did this took my journal."

In an uncharacteristically kind gesture, Alice Lambert put her arm around Anna and pulled her close, shushing her and patting her hair. "We will get it back for you. Everything will be just fine dear." She gestured to the orderlies to move in and clear the damage from her room while Alice led her to the nurses' station and sat her down. "Would you like a cup of tea?"

Nodding, Anna swiped at her tears with the sleeve of her sweater. One of the other nurses handed her a box of tissue and another handed her a piece of chocolate. "You look like you need this more than I do," the young blond said kindly.

"Thank you. I think you may be right." Anna popped the chocolate in her mouth and let it melt on her tongue. It had been a long time since she had had real chocolate, the kind that was so rich it tasted almost like salted coffee. Nurse Lambert handed her a cup of tea and sat with her while it cooled, the orderlies marching by with bits and pieces of Anna's belongings. It took them nearly an hour to clean the whole thing up, including the glass from a broken window no one had noticed at first. She watched as one of the maintenance men came trundling down the hall with his fix-it cart, two pieces of plywood and a drill balanced on top.

"They're going to have to board up that window tonight but it shouldn't be too bad. It's warm enough," Nurse Lambert reassured her. "They'll have it all good as new. You'll see."

When she was finally allowed back in her room her bed had been put back together and remade, her desk replaced with all her pens and pencils arranged neatly in a pretty flowered mug, and her clothing hung carefully in her closet. The books had been taken away, likely to be discarded given the amount of damage that had been done to them-- their spines had been broken, pages torn out, covers bent at wrong angles. Anna thought perhaps that was what angered her most about the vandalism, that and the disappearance of her journal of course.

"Let's give you a little something extra to sleep." Holding the remains of her tea, Anna waited for Alice to return with her medications, a double dose of sleeping pills on the side. She washed them down and finished off her tea, then handed the mug to Alice.

"Thank you for the tea. And thank you for getting them to fix all this." She looked around at her room, like new but now completely changed.

"Of course dear. Why don't you try to get some sleep and tomorrow we'll see if we can track down your journal."

Nodding, Anna went to her closet and pulled out her pajamas. She changed quickly and dove under her covers, pulling them up over her head. All she wanted to do at that moment was hide from the world, hide from the vandal who had tarnished the safety of her room. When Nurse Lambert had asked who could have done that level of damage, Anna's first thought had been perhaps that really was Peder she had seen hurrying away from her room just minutes before she discovered the mess. There was no question that Peder was capable of such a display, but why would he have done something like that?

The journal. Anna squeezed her eyes shut and pulled the blankets tight around her. He had snuck into her room and read the journal. That had to be it. There was more than enough written in there about him to make him angry, to make him snap even. And now she suspected that he had taken it and was likely holed up somewhere reading the rest of her private thoughts. She felt tears form in the corners of her eyes but she was too tired to cry; the extra dose of sleeping pills was making her woozy and rubbery, her eyes dry and heavy. Drifting off, the last thing she was aware of was the scrape of her door opening and footsteps approaching her bed.

After what seemed like hours-- or was it only minutes?- Anna opened her eyes and tried to roll over but she couldn't, then realized she was sitting up on something hard, no longer in her bed. She squeezed her eyes shut, then opened them slowly, letting them adjust slowly to the darkness so that she could just barely make out her surroundings. Looking down at the cracked tile floor coated in paint chips, she immediately knew she was in the old ward and she wasn't alone; she could hear someone breathing on the opposite side of the room.

"Ah, finally. She's awake." Peder's voice carried over to her on a tiny breeze that ruffled the curtains on the window, the one in which she had once sworn her mother had stood. The handprint was still there but now, in her more lucid mind, she knew that it was her own handprint on the glass, not that of a spirit or ghost.

"Peder, what…"

"Shh. Let me stop you right there. You know exactly what's happening and why I'm doing it. So don't bother with the inane questions." He was standing against the wall behind her somewhere and she heard him push off and walk towards her, the crunch of the paint under his feet like gunfire in the empty space. "So I have to say, I was pretty entertained by that journal of yours. Quite insightful."

Anna watched him circle her like a big cat circles its prey, his eyes glazed and angry, spit collecting in the corners of his mouth as he blew out each labored breath.

"Oh yes, very interesting, especially your analysis of me Dr. Gilman. Very insightful I have to say." He laughed, a harsh, biting sound that was tipping over into mania. "And I loved your adorable little checklist of reasons why you should keep me at arm's length. I'm surprised you didn't doodle little devil horns in the margins!"

It was then that Anna noticed her little brown journal dangling from his hand, his thumb keeping his page as he paced in front of her. "Let's see, now here's a good one, 'Peder is simply trying to manipulate me into trusting him, into letting my guard down, but Valerie says...' How about that, Valerie says, Valerie says," he stopped in front of her and bent down until he was at eye level. "If Valerie told you to jump off the roof of the hospital would you do it?" He screamed with laughter, showering Anna with spit and sweat, waving her journal in his flapping arms. "Of course you would!"

As he continued to hurl passages at her from her journal, Anna racked her brain trying to figure out how to get herself out of this predicament but he had used zip ties to lash her arms and legs to the chair and they were far enough away from the main building that she knew her screams would never be heard. Instead, she decided to try the path of reason.

"Peder, please don't lend any credence to that. I knew they were reading my journal. Harper had given it to Valerie and after she lectured me about you…"

"Oh please," Peder exploded. "And you call me manipulative. You can't fool me Anna Gilman. This is all you."

"It's not Peder, I swear. I told Valerie flat out that she couldn't tell me who I could and couldn't talk to…"

"Enough!" He screamed. "Enough. You know, I really did enjoy reading all this introspective, self-searching bullshit you wrote. You really know how to milk a lousy childhood, I'll give you that, but you have no idea how good you had it." Stopping his pacing, Peder stood in front of her and crossed his arms over his chest, her journal tucked under his elbow. "You want hard luck? My parents were both mentally ill, both drug addicts. I grew up on the streets of Lowell, literally running the streets until the lights came on at dusk. Then, and only then, was I allowed to come home. I found the only place I could get heat in the winter and air conditioning in the summer-- at the library. I read everything I could get my hands on, the classics, the modernists, the romantics. Joyce, Hemingway, Vonnegut."

Another chair appeared from the darkness and he swung it around to sit backwards, his chin resting on the back of the chair as he scrutinized his captive audience. "I read until I was able to graduate at the top of my class and get the hell away from my abusive parents who couldn't stay clean long enough to put a real meal on the table." He tilted his head and reached out to brush the hair out of her eyes, tucking it behind her ears like a lover would, letting his fingertips linger on her jaw line. "I went away to college and never looked back. Last I heard they were both in jail, or dead. Who cares."

Anna tried her best not to pull away from Peder's touch, not wanting to anger him even further, though her skin was crawling. "I'm sorry you had to go through that. Really I am."

"Do you know how many times I've heard 'I'm sorry' in my lifetime? The school nurses used to say it when I would come in with bruises and bloody noses. The cafeteria ladies would say it when I didn't have enough money for lunch. But then I was awarded valedictorian of my class and went on to Harvard. Ah! See? You didn't know that about me," he chuckled, noting the widening of her eyes. "Yes I'm an Ivy League graduate, a Harvard man. And I went on to teach at a crap public university because I started to fall apart at the seams. I started hearing things, and seeing things. Just like you."

"You're nothing like me!" Anna shouted back, unable to let the comparison between them go without comment. "And I am nothing like you! I may have seen things but at least I try my best to allow these people to help me. What do you do? You spend your time here harassing me, and trashing my room so you can steal my journal, ripping me apart for taking medications when you're so drugged up I'm surprised you even know your own name."

"Oh ho ho! The kitten has claws!" Peder sat back in mock surprise, pretending to be affronted by her outburst but she had played right into his hands and let him goad her into reacting. "Funny how you don't balk until I draw a comparison between your illness and mine. What's the matter Anna? Do you think you're better than I am? Because I have news for you. You're not. You're just as crazy, just as trapped, and just as lost."

Anna watched him rock forward in his chair, tipping onto the front legs with a wolfish grin. He was enjoying this little game, watching her and waiting for some kind of reaction from her. The zip ties chafed at her wrists as she moved, ever so subtly, trying to work herself free but she knew there was no real chance of breaking the ties.

"You know, in the end, I think I enjoyed the parts about your mother best. Especially when you started to remember what happened that night." Peder flippd the journal over and scanned the page in front of him. "Do you remember me telling you I vacationed in Niagara about a million years ago?"

Nodding, Anna tried to surreptitiously walk her chair away from Peder while he continued to run his eyes over the pages of her journal. "I remember it like it was yesterday. It was the first vacation I had ever taken on my own. I hitchhiked from Lowell to Buffalo, then walked across the bridge into Canada, back in the day when you didn't need much more than a school ID to cross the border."

He looked off into the distance, over Anna's shoulder, as if he was recalling a fond memory that he had been saving for dinner conversation or his memoirs. "It was a warm summer night and I was starving. All I wanted was a hot dog but I didn't have any money on me so I started asking passersby for change. A few people stopped and dug in their pockets, handing me whatever they could scrounge up; a few others told me to go piss up a rope. Eventually I had just enough for a soda, but not for a hot dog."

Anna watched him carefully as he looked back down at her journal, inching her chair farther away from him each time he glanced away. "You describe her so clearly, in her black tapered slacks and designer blouse. Her pointed toe shoes with the skinny heels. You don't say much about your father though. Why is that?"

"There's nothing to say," Anna answered quietly.

"Ah. Classic daddy issues. You must have been a cinch in therapy." Pulling a pack of cigarettes out of his pocket, Peder tapped one out and lit it, taking a long drag. "I got these from an orderly," he said, exhaling a cloud of white fog into the darkened room. "Right after I hit him over the head and knocked him out!" He cackled with delight and took another pull on the cigarette. "Want one?"

Anna shook her head and wrinkled her nose, leaning away from Peder. "You know, I always wondered why your father didn't go after your mother that night. He just sat inside the restaurant and muttered to himself."

"How do you know that?" Anna asked, unable to remember mentioning anything of the sort in her journal. "I don't think I said anything about him not going after her."

"Oh Anna, I told you I know everything there is to know about you. If I was him, I would have never let her leave, let alone let her wander the streets looking for you in your navy flowered dress with those little brown boots, the lace up ones that you loved so much."

"That was in my journal, that I know for sure. You just figured the rest out from everything I've written about my family."

Peder shook his head and made a "tsk" sound. "No Anna, I didn't. I already knew these things long before I got my hands on this," he said, waving her journal at her.

"How is that possible? If it wasn't in my journal then you would have had to have been there that night and that's impossible!" Anna heard the panic rising in her voice as she considered what she was saying. Was it really impossible?

"You know, some people never learn how to just be kind to others who aren't as well off as they are. That's something your mother really needed to work on." As Peder stood and tossed his chair to the side, Anna cringed at the sound of wood cracking against tile. "All I wanted was a hot dog and a drink. I had enough for the drink but not quite enough for the hot dog and when I asked her for change…" Peder spun on his heel and looked out the window, holding out his hands as if he was beseeching some invisible judge for his opinion. "When I asked her for change she tried to ignore me!"

"No, no. You couldn't have been there…" Anna whispered, tears gathering in the corners of her eyes as she realized what he was saying.

"Oh I was there," he said, moving closer to the window. He pressed his forehead against the glass and rocked it back and forth, his eyes closed. "I was there Anna. I was there and she wouldn't even acknowledge it. I know I looked a little rough but that was no reason to treat me like I was trash, like I didn't deserve even a minute of her time."

He couldn't possibly be telling the truth, yet how else would he have known what her mother was wearing that night, that her father sat in the restaurant and pouted rather than following his wife out into the unfamiliar streets? Letting his ravings wash over her, Anna realized he was still talking, still going on about her mother being rude and trying to ignore him.

"At first I was going to let it go; a woman alone on the street at night, and I had heard her calling out for Anna as she passed the souvenir shops and boutiques. It was obvious she was looking for someone, for you of course. But then she turned and looked right at me and said, 'I wouldn't give you the dirt from my heel' and kept walking." He laughed as if it still surprised him to this day that she could be so callous and unfeeling. "Well, that was enough for me. I got up good and close to her and I said, 'Hey lady, what did you say?' I expected her to back off but she didn't, she had some nerve your mother. She got right in my face and said, calm as can be, 'I said, I wouldn't give you the dirt off my heel. Now get out of my way'."

"I don't understand. Why would you get so angry over spare change?" Anna whispered.

"It wasn't the change I was angry about, precious Anna. I was angry about being dismissed, just like I had a thousand times before." Throwing her journal on the floor, Peder started to pace again, faster this time, his arms swinging wildly. "It was never easy for me Anna, no one wanted to help me or be nice to me for no reason. No one ever offered to listen to my problems. They passed me by and never looked back."

"My mother was just trying to find me in a strange city. And you...you *stabbed her* because she wouldn't give you money that you didn't earn and probably didn't deserve!" Anna heard her voice rising but her anger was so thick she didn't care that she was now yelling at him as her mother had done. "You murdered a stranger because you wanted a hot dog!" With a scream that ripped from the depths of her chest, Anna stood the best she could and swung the chair at the closest wall until she heard it splinter. She swung over and over while Peder stood, frozen in amazement, until she felt the back of the chair give way. Peder finally realized what she was doing and lunged forward but now that the chair was no longer in one piece, Anna was able to move a little more freely and she dodged him, smashing the chair against the wall again in the process.

"What is it you think you're going to do Anna?" He sang out as they played a wild, twisted game of musical chairs. "You're not getting out of here. Not now, not ever."

Smash. The leg of the chair splintered off and Anna shook her right foot to get the circulation back. "I'm going to break this chair to smithereens, then I'm going straight to Dr. Brown." The major flaw in that plan was that Peder was standing between her and the only way out of that room but in her blind rage she didn't notice that there was no egress.

"And what do you think Dr. Brown is going to do for you? Do you think he's going to believe the ravings of a delusional woman with a history of spinning tales?" Peder danced in front of her as she bobbed the other way. "Let's say he does believe you, just for the fun of it, what is he going to do? Don't you think I've figured out my escape route by now? I'll be long gone by the time you run to the man behind the curtain."

Slam. Anna rammed the chair into wall one final time, breaking its spine and sending shards of wood flying across the room. There was no way she was going to free herself of it completely but at least she could now stand upright. However, the moment she drew herself up, Peder reached out and slapped her hard across the face.

"Did you really think this little stunt with the chair would do you any good at all? I'm smarter than that my friend."

Stunned, Anna stood for a moment with her mouth sagging open, a string of drool dripping from her chin as pain radiated through her jaw. "You son of a bitch…" she muttered, straightening up. "You are a sorry excuse for a human being. You can't get your way so you damage and maim. What a sad, pathetic man you are."

The moment the words were out of her mouth, Peder's left hand snaked out and hit her on the other side of her face. "You know Anna, you might want to consider shutting your fool mouth. Like it or not, I have you backed into a corner, quite literally, and making me angry isn't such a good idea."

"I don't care. I'll go down fighting if that's what it comes to." Another blow landed on her ear, leaving it ringing with pain. "You're a murderer. A coward, and a murderer." He lashed out again, catching the corner of her eye and she saw stars as her vision swam.

"Your mother deserved what she got!" He roared, bringing his fist up and into her ribs, then he leaned close and bent so that he was eye level with her. She tried to focus on him, on his dark and empty eyes blazing with hate, but her head swam and she was seeing double. "She never even saw my knife," he whispered. "I pulled it out and sunk it into her gut right here." He jabbed his finger between her ribs where a bruise was already forming, she could feel it. Wincing in pain, Anna tried to pull away from him but he grabbed the back of her head and twined his fingers in her hair, yanking her forward. "I sunk that blade right between the bones and into her heart."

Anna sobbed and spat on the ground, a wad of blood landing in the dust. "You're a monster! A monster!"

"Yes, and you let this monster in!" He cackled with delight at the look of pure horror on her face, knowing he had scored a masterful blow. "You let this monster kiss you, to convince you to drop your guard." He whipped her head back and wrapped his other hand around her throat. "And now this monster is going to send you straight to your mother."

As his grip tightened on her throat, Anna's mind began to race. It was not her life that flashed before her eyes, but a rallying cry, an image of her mother being stabbed to death and left to die on the sidewalk like an animal. She reared back and brought her forehead crashing down on the bridge of Peder's nose as hard as she could.

Blood exploded from his nose and his hands flew up to protect himself from another blow as he staggered back. Anna flew by him, ramming him with her shoulder as she passed, knocking him to the floor. She rushed out of the room and out into the hallway where she was suddenly blind in the darkness, stumbling and tripping over floor tiles, but she pushed herself to keep moving. She could hear Peder behind her, roaring with anger, and she knew she didn't have much of a head start with pieces of the broken chair still dangling from her limbs.

"Get back here you witch!" Peder's voice was muffled by pain but was also closer than she had hoped. She blindly charged, one footstep at a time, towards safety and freedom until she heard an ear splitting explosion and felt her legs give out from under her as she fell down and down and down. When she finally stopped falling, she realized she had landed on the floor below, the breath knocked out of her, and her leg bent under her at an odd angle. Suddenly Peder's face appeared through the hole above her and his maniacal laughter carried down to her where she lay, completely immobile, completely exposed. "That's what you get for running from me." And he disappeared.

Minutes later she heard his footsteps coming for her. She tried to move but the pain was just too great. There was no escaping him now and so instead, Anna laid her head back and stared up into nothingness. "I'm sorry mom. I'm sorry." She closed her eyes and let the pain wash over her as she felt hands slide under her and lift her gently.

Chapter 23

"Help! Help us! She's fallen through the floor in the old ward. I think her leg's broken." When she came to again, Anna heard a voice that sounded very much like Peder's yelling for help. Opening her eyes, she looked around and realized she was still being held aloft and when she turned to look at the face of her rescuer, she gasped.

"Peder, what are you doing?"

He looked down at her and smiled, a cold, evil smile that didn't reach his eyes. "You know, when I looked down at you from that hole, it occurred to me that, while killing you would certainly be entertaining, there were far better ways to destroy you."

It suddenly dawned on Anna's aching brain what he was doing and she began to struggle, ignoring the searing pain in every inch of her body. "No! No! He did this, he did this to me!" He tightened his grip on her until she cried out in pain.

"I found her lying in the debris," Peder said, feigning concern as an orderly approached with a coterie of nurses. "She was delusional, kept muttering something about me killing her mother. You have to help her." He looked down at her, all care and concern, then winked, ever so slightly.

She went mad in his arms, screaming and rocking from side to side, her broken leg dangling as she panicked. "No, no. Don't believe him! He's a murderer! He's lying!" The orderlies took her as someone appeared with a stretcher and a vial of something nasty looking.

One of the nurses had pulled Peder away from the chaos and was patting him on the arm, reassuring him that Anna would be just fine as soon as they got her medicated and tended to her leg. By now she was sobbing, not from pain but from the fear of being misunderstood. How could they think that he had saved her? How could he have them all fooled? Tears streamed from her eyes as she lay on the gurney, the orderlies strapping her wrists to the bed rails as they wheeled her towards the infirmary. "You can't believe him!" she screamed. "He brought me to that room, he tied me to a chair. He hit me over and over. Can't you see the bruises on my face?"

"Honey you've had a bad fall," one of the nurses said, leaning over her as they wheeled down the hall. "We'll get you fixed up right as rain." She looked over at Peder adoringly. "Thank goodness that young man found you when he did!"

"You don't understand! He isn't...." The nurse shushed her as the powerful sedative kicked in and wiped her consciousness clean. When she woke again it was mid-morning and she was in the infirmary, alone in her bed behind a white curtain, her leg in traction. She was still restrained and could not sit up but she could see her toes, high in the air, encased in a heavy plaster cast; the fall had obviously done some damage.

Nurses came and went, checking her vital signs and giving her medication. Each time she tried to tell them what Peder had done, they gave her the same pitying look and an extra shot of sedative. No one believed her and that was exactly what he had known would happen.

By late afternoon Anna was awake and ravenous, salivating as a nurse wheeled in a tray of food. "Nurse Lambert said you like tea so I brought you that as well," she said undoing the wrist restraints so she could eat. "Let me know if I can get you anything else or if you start to have any pain." She smiled sweetly and backed out the door. "Oh, I almost forgot. You have a visitor!"

Peder's smiling face appeared in Anna's doorway as he thanked the nurse for showing him in. "How are you, you poor thing. Look at you! You're all broken!"

"Don't you come near me. I'll scream. I swear I'll scream."

Making a tsk-ing sound, Peder wagged his finger at her as he approached her bedside. "Now now. Is that any way to treat a friend who's come to check on you?"

"Nurse! Nurse! Help me! Get him out of here!" Anna began to scream and bang her wrist restraints against the bed rails. "He's a murderer! Get him out of here!"

Two nurses rushed in, pushing Peder aside as they hurried to give Anna another sedative. "Relax," they cooed in unison, as if they'd practiced.

"I'm so sorry," Peder sighed, putting on a look of worry that Anna knew *was* practiced. "I must have reminded her of her trauma yesterday. I just wanted to check on her but she's still stuck in this delusion that I murdered her mother."

"It's alright dear," the older nurse said, rubbing his shoulder in sympathy. "She'll be just fine."

Drifting off once again, Anna woke to a hand on hers and she jerked away only to realize it was Valerie sitting next to her. "Welcome back to the living. You gave us quite the scare."

"It wasn't me Valerie. It was Peder. He…"

"Now, none of that." Valerie sighed and looked away from Anna, then back to her bruised and contorted face. "He said he found you in that abandoned room again, talking to yourself."

Anna squeezed her eyes shut and willed herself not to cry, not now. She had to convince Valerie that she wasn't imagining things this time. "You told me not to be taken in by him, not believe his charm, that inside he was dangerous. Do you remember that?" Valerie nodded slowly. "Well now I'm asking you to take your own advice. Don't trust what he's telling you. It's just a manipulation."

Valerie looked hard at her, as if she was trying to see through her, see the truth inside her head. "That could very well be true, but why would he risk taking you from your room, then go so far as to confess to murdering your mother, only to turn around and try to fool us all into believing it was in your head?"

"Why wouldn't he?" Anna tried to sit up, forgetting that she was still strapped to the bed. "Think about it. He's crazy, crazier than most of us, and you and Harper both said he was prone to violence."

"Yes, but a simple assault charge is a far cry from a murder."

"Valerie, he already has is out for me. He thinks we share some secret bond that's all in his head." She could see that Valerie still wasn't buying it, but she was certainly considering it. "Listen, he was able to tell me details of that night that no one else knows, including what my mother was wearing that night. He even knew that my father didn't leave the restaurant to go after her." Anna took a deep breath and told her the most important thing. "Valerie, he knew how many times she had been stabbed, a detail that was never released."

Valerie sighed. "Well now it's your word against his. And he's saying he said no such thing, that you're making this all up."

"Isn't there some way to check?" Anna pleaded frantically. "Can't you find out if any of what he said about Niagara is true? There must be a record of him crossing the border."

"I'm sure, but that would take quite a bit of time to check on Anna." Valerie threw up her hands in exasperation. "It's not like I can just pick up the phone and call border control."

The tears Anna had been trying so hard to hold back slipped down her cheeks unchecked. "Valerie please. You have to. I'm not imagining this."

Standing, Valerie smoothed down the front of her shirt and picked at a piece of lint on her cuff. "I'll see what I can do. No promises."

The next to visit her was Harper who came bearing yet another cup of hot tea and a pile of books from the library. "They managed to replace the ones that were destroyed in your room so I grabbed them when they came in." Setting the books down, she put the tea on Anna's bed tray and undid her restraints. "Those can stay off now, as long as you keep it together and stop yelling at people," she said with a smirk.

"Listen Harper," she started, trying to keep her voice steady. "You have to believe me. I know Valerie doesn't but you have to. You know me better than anyone."

Harper rested her elbows on her knees and leaned forward, looking down at the floor. "I do know you better than anyone. I also know that you just spent the last year living as if you were a nursing intern instead of a patient, and you had no idea what was reality."

"You saw my room after it was trashed." Anna swiped at her still damp eyes. "Do you think *I* did that?"

Without giving her an answer, Harper sighed and shook her head. "No, I don't think you did."

"When they put my room back together, the only thing we couldn't find was my journal. When Peder took me to that room, he had it. He took it and read the whole thing." Harper still hadn't looked up but Anna could tell she was listening. ":Look, he was smart enough to know that the violation of my space would stress me out." Harper looked doubtful, not certain where Anna was going with her diatribe. "He knew the nurses would give me an extra dose of sleeping pills so he could come back for me in the middle of the night and I would be too out of it to do anything. When I came to he was pacing and ranting, he was so angry about everything I had written about him."

"What had you written?"

"That Valerie was right, that he was manipulative and crazy. I had finally realized that he just wanted me to give in to him and trust him so he could have the upper hand."

"And did you?"

Anna nodded miserably. "For a little while I did. I thought maybe Valerie had been wrong about him and that he had grown, changed. I thought it was a reflection of my own illness, that if he could get his schizophrenia under control then I could do the same with my own illness. But once I had my own moods under control I realized I was just fooling myself into thinking that he was safe to be around."

"So you wrote all this in your journal, which he read."

"Yes and it was apparently the tipping point for him. He brought me to that room and he was out of his mind, reading passages out of my journal aloud, saying that I had betrayed him by letting you read it." Anna sank back into her pillows, exhausted.

"He kept saying he knew everything there was to know about me. I didn't understand what he meant until the other night."

"You mean he said it more than once?"

"Yes," Anna nodded. "He said it that day in the pharmacy. He said, 'I know everything about you Anna Gilman."

"And what he meant was that he knew everything about your mother's murder."

Anna nodded again, her hands balled into fists at her sides. "I swear to you Harper. I am as lucid as possible right now. I've been on my medication for weeks now and I've just spent two days tied to a bed. I know exactly what's going on, someone just has to believe me."

Harper rubbed her hands together and chewed her bottom lip. "Ok here's what I'm going to do. I'm going to have the orderlies toss Peder's room. If he has your journal, then we'll know he's not being as honest as everyone thinks."

"But what if he never even grabbed the journal after rescuing me?"

Shrugging, Harper looked up at Anna, her eyes sad. "Then we can't prove anything. For all we know, you put it there yourself."

That slammed her right in the chest, the thought that they might doubt her to that extreme, to think that she was delusional to the point that she would try to frame Peder when it was the other way around. She hoped against hope that they would find her journal somewhere in his room or on his person; it felt like this was her only hope, her only chance to prove that Peder was the one who was lying, but she also knew it was a feeble hope at best. What were the chances that he had gone back to that room to retrieve the journal after tossing it to the floor? Slim, that's what.

After Harper left her, she lay in bed and tried to finish the book on the Fox Sisters. As she read, she grew more and more embarrassed at her own willingness to accept everything Peder had said at face value. She had even been willing to entertain the thought that she was being haunted by some wayward asylum spirit. He had realized that she was actively deluded and he had taken advantage of her weakened state to make her trust him. She had been a fool and she had played right into his hands.

By the time Harper got back, Anna had given up on the book, tossing it on the bedside table. This time she had come with Dr. Brown in tow. "Anna, do me a favor and tell Dr. Brown everything you told me about Peder. From the beginning."

"Like the very beginning?"

"Everything," Harper nodded. "Right from the moment he stepped off the van."

Anna took a deep breath and recounted the entire saga for the old man with the graying moustache and protruding belly. She told him about every moment with Peder-- every look, every conversation, every encounter, even the strange look he had given her as he had gotten off the van. Then there was the Christmas gift and his unreasonable reaction to the whole thing, his bizarre attachment to her and his refusal to accept that there was nothing between them.

"Dr. Westcott tells me there was also a run in during that storm?" Brown interrupted.

"Yes there was. Peder was angry with me because he thought I had betrayed him somehow even though I had no idea how."

Brown was frowning now. "Alright. Go on."

She went on, telling him about the incident in the pharmacy and Peder's strange declaration about knowing her. Finally Anna told him about her room being trashed and her journal going missing.

"This journal, what did it look like?"

"It was small, brown leather with a strap to keep it closed." Anna fiddled with her fingers. "Valerie gave it to me when I first got here."

He glanced over his shoulder and shot Harper a look, then pulled a crumpled piece of paper out of his pocket and handed it to her. "We didn't find your journal but we did find this." Anna carefully unfolded the sheet and smoothed it out on her knee. It was a page from her journal, the one where she had listed her reasons to stay away from Peder.

"Where was it?"

"Under his mattress," Harper answered.

"So that's it then. You believe me."

Dr. Brown hesitated, then took the paper back from her. "We've put in a call to the Royal Canadian Mounted Police. We're trying our best to confirm that Peder Roderick was in the area when your mother was murdered. Until we do, we need you to sit tight and we'll keep him isolated."

"What about me?"

"What about you?" He asked, looking puzzled.

"How will you keep me safe?"

Harper stepped in front of Brown and took Anna's hand. "There will be at least one orderly outside your room every minute and the entire infirmary staff is under strict orders not to allow Peder anywhere near you."

In her head she was thinking there wasn't much that could stop Peder from getting to her, but out loud she said, "Thank you. I appreciate you both considering what I'm saying."

Brown nodded and tried for a smile which came out as a half grimace, as if he didn't do it very often, but he patted her on the shoulder and reassured her that everything was under control, then walked out the door leaving Harper standing over her.

"Shove over cripple." Harper gently lowered herself onto the edge of the bed and leaned back next to her as if they were having a sleepover. "I'm sorry about all this."

"As long as you're starting to believe me that's really all that matters to me. I couldn't handle it if you doubted me."

"I'm going to be honest, I didn't believe you at first. It sounded pretty far-fetched."

Anna turned to face her and looked into her eyes. "What changed your mind?"

Sighing, Harper stared up at the ceiling. "It was the pharmacist. He repeated what Peder had said about knowing everything about you. He said it was the way Peder said it, like a soap opera stalker."

"That's what it feels like. I wouldn't be surprised at this point if he had an evil twin brother that came back from the dead."

The two women laughed and Anna relaxed a little, knowing that the ball was in motion and they were finally starting to understand what was happening. "Thank you for believing me, no matter how you came to it."

"No problem."

That night, as she lay in her bed listening to the machines around her beeping and humming, Anna wondered just how safe she really was here. Peder was a determined man, evidenced by his careful planning in taking her from her room. She hugged the blankets to herself and tried her best to fall asleep but even after a sedative her mind was still racing. Her back was beginning to ache from laying in the same position day after day and she was beyond bored. The cast that went from hip to toe itched terribly, but thankfully she was shot full of enough pain medication that the leg just ached dully.

When she finally began to drift off, she caught the motion of a shadow moving near the doorway, a shadow that seemed to be finding its way into the room slowly and quietly. "Hello? Who's there?" Anna propped herself up on her elbows and peered into the darkness that was barely split by the emergency lights out in the hallway. The infirmary was a slightly older ward, the lights dimmer and the rooms darker, the nurses' station farther away. There were also three separate ways to get to the infirmary without having to pass said nurses, which meant that someone sneaking into her room could have done so without arousing any sort of suspicion.

Still sensing movement, Anna tried to see into the dark and listened hard, thinking she could hear someone breathing in the corner, but unsure whether or not it was her imagination, but as the breathing drew closer, she knew for certain that there was someone there and she readied herself to scream, but just as the figure in the room made it to her bedside, the lights flashed on and there was a flurry of action as an orderly tackled her visitor. They engaged in a heated scuffle right there on the floor, the orderly pinning him on his face and twisting his arm behind his back. Anna recognized the sound of Peder's voice as he lashed out, trying to fight the orderly the best he could.

Pulling Peder to his feet, the orderly wrenched his arm up between his shoulder blades until he yelled out in pain. He seethed in the orderly's grasp, sweat rolling down his forehead and into his eyes. "You'll never be free of me," he screamed as they dragged him away. "You'll never be free!"

Clutching her chest, Anna tried to steady her breathing and stop her heart from pounding. "What the hell was that?" Anna asked as Harper shook her head in dismay. "How did he get in here?"

"He knocked out the orderly we had posted outside his room," she replied, seeing the question in Anna's eyes. "I had a gut feeling there was something wrong tonight and when I went to check on Mr. Roderick, the orderly was out cold in the hallway. I just had a hunch he would make his way here."

"I can't believe he did that."

Harper shrugged. "I can't believe it took him this long to be honest." She pulled up a chair and sat next to Anna, reaching out to fluff the pillows behind her head.

"You say it like you were hoping something like this would happen."

"Well," Harper hesitated. "I was hoping. The page from the journal just wasn't enough so we made sure he overheard me scolding a particular orderly for not paying better attention to his job, falling asleep on the night shift. Then a few days later, I posted that orderly outside his room." Chuckling, Harper shook her head. "I didn't count on Peder knocking Ben out though. I suppose I'll have to give him an extra paid vacation day for that one."

Stunned, Anna began to laugh with Harper, her bumps and bruises hurting with the effort. "You planned all of this? Just to trap him?"

"Look. there was no way the Canadian border control was going to give a rat's ass about a tiny mental hospital in the middle of nowhere Massachusetts. This was the best way."

"What's going to happen to him now?"

"Now," Harper sighed. "Now he sits in isolation on the violent ward until we can get him to incriminate himself. Until then, I'm sitting with you." Pulling out a deck of cards, Harper dragged the bed tray over and started to shuffle. "Crazy Eights?"

They passed hours playing cards, drinking tea, and talking about everything under the sun. Anna was still feeling a bit foolish about having been fooled by Peder, but Harper reminded her that sometimes attraction was blind and to be grateful that she came to her senses. Harper told Anna about a disastrous blind date she had gone on a couple days before and Anna laughed heartily as Harper recounted the end of the night indecision of kiss, handshake, or hug; she described it as an embarrassing adult version of rock, paper, scissors.

Finally it was time for lights out and Harper kicked up her feet on another chair, settling in for the night. "Harper, you don't have to do this. Stay with me overnight I mean."

"Yes I do. Who else is going to kick his ass if he comes back?" With a smirk she closed her eyes and they both drifted off.

It was early the next morning before Valerie and Dr. Brown stopped in as well. "He's in isolation, in the violent ward, which I'm sure you already know," Valerie said, gesturing at Harper. "We went after him all night and he finally cracked." She looked sad as she came to the side of the bed. "Anna, I'm so sorry I doubted you. He confessed to everything, in a roundabout way."

"Oh thank God." Anna sank back on her pillows and immediately burst into tears as she realized that Peder had admitted to everything and was now stuck behind a locked door with nothing but a tiny four by four window. "So he took responsibility for all of it?"

"Well," Valerie and Brown traded glances. "He hasn't said anything about your mother's death. He admits to trashing your room and taking your journal, and he owned up to taking you from your room and pretending to be your rescuer when you fell. But he hasn't mentioned your mother."

Of course he hadn't. It was the one weapon he had left against her and he was going to hold onto it as long as he could. "What will happen to him now?"

"He faces another formal assault charge," Brown cut in. "And it'll be a very long time before he leaves the violent ward. At this point, I don't think he'll ever see the outside world again unless it's to transfer to a jail cell."

That should have been a comfort to Anna, a neat resolution to the problem of Peder Roderick but she wanted more. She wanted answers. "Can I go see him?"

"Whatever for?" Valerie asked, her face twisting in shock.

"There are some questions to which I need answers that only he can give." Anna sat up best she could. "I'd like to ask them before you lock him up and throw away the key."

Valerie was about to object but Harper interrupted her. "I think it's a good idea Nurse Martin. It might be just the closure Anna needs in order to move on with her own treatment. Don't you agree?" She glanced over at Dr. Brown as well, including him peripherally in the decision.

"I suppose you're right," Valerie conceded after a moment of thought. "I can't see what harm it could cause as long as you have a steel door between you." She sighed and shook her head, this decision obviously made against her better judgement. "But not until you're out of traction, obviously. I don't want you risking your physical health either."

"Yes ma'am," Anna said with a smile and a mock salute. She appreciated Valerie's level of concern and was grateful that she was putting Anna's need for information above her own lack of trust in the idea of putting Anna face to face with Peder.

"You rest." Turning to go, Valerie turned and glanced over her shoulder at Anna. "You've come long way Miss Gilman. I'm glad to see you're not stopping now."

With a nod, Dr. Brown followed Valerie out of the room and she was once again alone with Harper. "I can't believe they agreed to that."

"Neither can I," Harper replied. It had been a shot in the dark, asking them for time with Peder but Anna knew she had no other choice, she had to talk to him and get him to confess to killing her mother. It was the only way she could feel some peace and finally wipe away a bit of the guilt she had carried for so many years.

"I wonder how long I'll have to wait."

"The infirmary nurse said you'll likely be out of traction in a week. I promise we'll get you to him as soon as we can."

That night Anna slept soundly and dreamlessly for the first time in years. There was comfort in knowing that no one would be coming for her in the night and that she was one step closer to knowing the whole truth about her mother's death. It was a liberating feeling, a relief of pressure Anna had never thought possible and she was grateful to have stumbled, even as she lay there with her leg in the air. When her week in traction was up, Harper was there, as promised, to wheel her over to the violent ward.

"Up you go." An orderly helped Harper lower Anna into a wheelchair then covered her with a blanket and tucked a pillow behind her. "Might as well ride comfortably, right?"

Anna nodded, her mind racing and unfocused. She had rehearsed the speech she would give Peder over and over, but it still sounded trite, begging him to do the right thing and allow her mother to rest in the peace of knowing her killer had been found. She imagined him laughing at her, pointing and jeering, but still she had to try. When they finally wheeled her in front of Peder's door, a slot in the middle open so she could talk to him, she suddenly didn't know what to say.

"Well, well. Look who came back for more!" Peder sneered as his face appeared in the slot. He was kneeling on the floor so that he could see Anna through the slot and make eye contact, a trick that was meant to disarm her; it had worked. She was suddenly terrified to be sitting here, an arm's length away from him even though they were separated by three inches of metal and a heavy padlock. "What do you want princess?"

It took her a moment to find her voice and when she finally spoke it cracked under the weight of what she wanted to say. Finally she whispered, "I want you to admit to killing my mother, just like you did the night I broke my leg."

Peder pretended to think about it for a moment, then rocked forward to press his face against the slot so that the only think Anna could see were his eyes. "Now why would I want to do a thing like that?"

"Because she deserves justice. And I deserve some peace."

"Oh, do you now? And what about me, what do I deserve?"

Anna pushed herself up in her chair and brought her own face as close to the slot as she could. "You deserve a needle in your arm you bastard." She spat at him through the slot and he reared back as if she had hit him.

Wiping the moisture from his cheek, Peder looked down at his hands as if he had been doused with acid. "You bitch. There's no way in hell I'm going to tell you anything. Besides, no one would ever take my word for it because I'm crazy!" he shouted and began to dance around his cell and make bizarre faces. "I'm crazy, crazy, crazy! Boo!" he yelled as he stuck his nose in the slot, making Anna jump. "Ha. Scared ya didn't I.

Anna watched in fascination as Peder unraveled right in front of her, slapping his palms against the walls and yelling obscenities. He ranted and raved but never once did he speak of her mother loudly enough for anyone but her to hear. "This is my greatest revenge Anna, knowing that you will never be able to prove that I murdered your mother. You alone have heard my confession and now you will have to carry it with you the rest of your life, like a noose around your neck, just waiting to snap your neck under the pressure."

He turned away from her and picked something up off his bed, then turned to face her once more with his arms outstretched like Christ on the cross, his head flung back, teeth bared. "It will torment you, and it will eat you alive, but you won't be able to do a damned thing about it Anna Gilman!"

With that he drew his hand across his throat, a bloom of fresh, red-black blood beading from ear to ear. Anna looked down and saw the piece of jagged glass he was holding in his hand, a point like a tiger's claw on the end. By the time Anna found her voice and yelled for the orderlies, Peder had already sunk to his knees, the front of his gray shirt soaked with blood. He must have sharpened that point so that he could cut deeply enough to sever an important artery. The orderlies came running at the sound of Anna's screams, unlocking Peder's door and lifting him onto his bed.

Anna caught a glimpse of him lying, prostrate on his bed, his left arm hanging off the side of the mattress, his eyes growing dim and his jaw slack. "How the hell did he get a piece of glass?" One of the orderlies had pried it from his fingers and was inspecting the dried blood on its razor sharp edge. "Jesus Christ." The other orderly, who had been trying to resuscitate Peder, sat back on the foot of the bed and dropped his bloody hands in his lap.

"We lost him," he said, looking over his shoulder and realizing that Anna had watched the entire event. "Get her out of here. She shouldn't be seeing this."

As they wheeled her away she took one last glance at Peder's motionless face, yet she would swear she saw him wink.

Chapter 24

The day Valerie left Westborough to return to Northampton someone circulated a card for the entire staff to sign, then left it on her desk on top of a banker's box. She worked slowly, packing the few things she wanted to take with her; her journals had already been boxed up and shipped to her new address. As she carefully laid her desk organizer in the box, Harper Westcott appeared in the door, knocking lightly as she came in.

"So this is it," she said with a grimace. "You're going back to Northampton?"

Valerie nodded. She wasn't much for goodbyes and had been hoping to avoid the small talk and niceties that went with a public sendoff but now it seemed she had no choice. "It is. So much for retirement," she deadpanned as she emptied her pen cup and wrapped her Smith College coffee mug in some tissue before adding it to the box.

"Why'd you say yes then?" Harper perched on the arm of Valerie's couch and regarded her curiously. "Why not just tell them to shove it and continue on as planned?"

Shrugging, Valerie looked around her office which was now nearly bare in spite of the fact that she had only filled the box halfway. "Northampton is where it all started."

"All what?"

She shrugged again and suddenly looked sad. "My life."

Before she left she went up to the chronic ward in the Childs Building where she was greeted by young, fresh-faced clinical nurses and burly orderlies who looked like they wrestled grizzlies in their spare time.

"Can I help you?" The receptionist was the only person who looked as if she belonged in that building with her cat's eye glasses and outdated hairstyle. She reminded Valerie of the woman she had interviewed with at Northampton.

"Valerie Martin. I'm here to see Anna Gilman. She is...was my patient."

"Let me see if I can get ahold of the attending." She turned away and pressed a button on the beige rotary dial phone in front of her. "Dr. Carruthers? There's a Valerie Martin here to see... yes. Ok. I'll tell her you're on your way." Hanging up the receiver she turned back to Valerie. "Dr. Carruthers will be right down."

Valerie nodded her thanks and leaned against the closest wall waiting for Dick Carruthers to come down for her. She knew him well, had started at Westborough the same time he did. He had transferred in from Grafton the same time she had come from Northampton. He appeared around the corner, holding out his hand for Valerie to shake.

"I hear this is the end of the road for you. Is it true?"

"Not quite," Valerie sighed. "I'm heading back to Northampton to wrap up some paperwork for them first. Should only be a few months. Then I'll take my retirement." She chucked him in the arm. "What about you? Aren't you getting close to the end too?"

"Two more years. Then I'm going sailing and never coming back," he said, laughing heartily.

Valerie followed him up the stairs and down a narrow yellow and brown hallway. "How is she?"

"The same." He stepped aside to let Valerie pass, heading straight for Anna's room. "She still hasn't said a word to anyone.

Her leg is finally healed but she shows no interest in getting out of bed. Unfortunately we can't force her if she won't communicate with us. We can't risk an injury going undetected."

"Understood." Stepping into Anna's room, Valerie steeled herself for the girl's skeletal appearance. Not only had Anna stopped speaking, she barely ate and she had lost a frightening amount of weight. She knew the medical team was considering implanting a feeding tube if she didn't start eating on her own. "Anna?" Valerie placed herself directly in Anna's line of sight but the girl's milky eyes didn't even flicker with an ounce of recognition. "I came to say goodbye to you. I'm going back to Northampton."

Valerie watched for some sign that Anna had heard her but there was no reaction, she just continued to stare off into space, her mouth slack, a string of drool escaping from the corner of her lips. "Listen, we finally heard back from the Canadian border patrol. They were able to confirm that Peder crossed into Niagara the night of your mother's death. It's not a smoking gun by any means but it certainly throws some guilt his way."

Sitting on the edge of the bed, Valerie took Anna's cold, thin hand in hers and held it tight. "I'm so sorry that this happened to you, all of it. I wish I could take it all back for you and make Peder face the sentence he deserved." They had buried Peder in a pine box in the potter's field at the edge of the hospital's Pine

Grove Cemetery. It was more than he deserved, Valerie thought. Then Valerie had made the phone call she had been dreading.

"Sarah?"

"Yes?" The voice on the other end sounded so much older, though Valerie realized, so must she.

"This is Valerie Martin at Westborough."

"Oh hi, how are you?" Sarah Tessier sounded wary, knowing that a call from the hospital likely meant less than positive news.

"I'm well. Listen, I don't know how to tell you this but we've had an incident here." She took a deep breath and launched into an explanation of things that had been heavily edited by the hospital's board, leaving out some of the more salacious details that might have placed fault at the feet of the asylum. "Anna's being transferred to the chronic ward tomorrow."

"Why?" She could hear the strain in Sarah's voice, the years of caring for her mentally ill niece all gathered in the strength-- or lack of- in her voice.

"She hasn't spoken a word since the incident with Mr. Roderick."

"Not to anyone? Not even Dr. Westcott?"

"No one. She's been heavily traumatized by this and we can't seem to break through to her." Valerie leaned back in her chair and closed her eyes. "And Sarah, I'm leaving soon."

"What do you mean you're leaving?"

"Well, I was supposed to retire but instead I'm going back to Northampton."

"Is that where you're from?" She could tell Sarah was struggling to keep the conversation going.

"It is. And it's where I started my career. I'll work there for a few more months before leaving the department entirely."

"Who's going to care for Anna?"

"She'll be transferred into the care of a good friend of mine, Dr. Richard Carruthers." It was times like these when she wished she was a smoker. "She'll be well taken care of Sarah, I promise."

Valerie hoped Sarah would come to visit soon and told her as much. Anna needed as many people by her side as possible to help her recover, if that was what was to be. Valerie hoped that some distance from the incident with Peder might help Anna recover, but she told Sarah there were no guarantees. She thanked Valerie quietly and hung up, leaving Valerie listening to the dial tone, unable to put the phone down. She liked Sarah very much and she admired everything she had done for Anna. Taking a teenager into her home couldn't have been easy, let alone one who had suffered so much trauma. Then to have to bring her to a psychiatrist and have her diagnosed as bipolar had to have been an even bigger blow to their already fragile existence. Yet Sarah had borne up admirably, getting Anna through high school, then college, and eventually sending her off to graduate school.

Even though Anna didn't make it through her Master's program, getting there had still been quite an accomplishment. Valerie had always hoped that one day Anna would go back to UMASS and finish her degree, perhaps even find a job at a state hospital or on a psych ward somewhere. Anna had a big heart and a generous nature; she would have made a great nurse. Now her future was anybody's guess but Valerie promised herself she would always hold out hope. As she sat with Anna and willed her to show some signs of recognition, hope was all she had.

"I'm going to miss you Anna. You made such great strides and I know you can do it again." Her touch had warmed the skin on Anna's hand but the rest of her was still cold. "Honey, I know you're still in there and I know you can hear me. You can't give up now. You have to promise me you won't give up, not like this." Valerie sighed and felt tears begin to pool on her bottom lids. She leaned forward and whispered, "If you give up now, then he wins. This is what he wanted."

She squeezed Anna's hand one last time and bent over to hug her goodbye but her body remained rigid in Valerie's arms. Wiping her eyes, Valerie turned to leave and bumped into Harper who held a bouquet of flowers and a book.

"I come and read to her as often as I can," she said, tilting the book so Valerie could see the cover. "She told me once that she loved Agatha Christie mysteries so that's what I bring her."

"I'm sure she appreciates it, somewhere deep inside of that shell of hers." Valerie smiled and touched Harper's arm, then ducked out of the room; she had a train to catch.

Chapter 25

Once Anna was confined to the chronic ward, Sarah Tessier sold her house in Lackawanna and moved to Massachusetts, taking a small apartment in Westborough so that she could be closer to her niece. She visited her every Sunday morning without fail, twice in a week if there was a holiday, though Anna never showed any sign that she was aware of her aunt's presence. Sarah fell into something of a routine with her visits, first telling Anna about that morning's sermon; she had taken to going to church after Anna's first major break. She said that going to church allowed her to rail at God in a place where she felt He had a better chance of hearing. Then she would step out of the room for a few minutes while the nurses gave Anna her medications, taking the opportunity to check in with Dr. Carruthers, though the conversation didn't change much from week to week.

"Has there been anything?" Sarah would ask.

Dr. Carruthers would simply shake his head sadly. "Nothing. I'm so sorry Miss Tessier." And he would go about his business checking in with the other patients. She couldn't blame him for his lack of optimism. It was, after all, the chronic ward.

After getting herself a cup of coffee in the small visitors' kitchen, Sarah would then sit with Anna for hours at a time, telling her stories of growing up with Teresa, laughing alone at her tales. Sometimes she would get tired of talking to herself and she would just sit and read, one hand resting lightly on top of Anna's. When she left, she always hoped Anna would watch her go, maybe give a wave or a nod, but she never did.

When they had cleaned out Anna's room in the main ward, they had found the carefully wrapped pile of letters Sarah had given her when she went away to school, the ones from Teresa's first love. One day she brought the letters with her and gently worked one out of the pack. Unfolding the scrap of yellowing paper, Sarah began to read the letter aloud to Anna, all her mother's hopes and joys, finally shared with her. The letters were full of declarations of love and a happiness that only came with the first blush of true romance. Sarah had forgotten just how happy her sister had been back then, before Malcolm. But of course if she hadn't married Malcolm, Sarah wouldn't have had Anna.

As much as she missed her sister, and for as much as she regretted the way things had come to an end, she was grateful for the time she had with her niece, watching her grow into an intelligent young woman with a curious spirit. In her attic at home she had added some Anna's drawings and poems to the box full of mementos that she kept-- pieces of her favorite people. It saddened her to think that the two most important women in her life had been reduced to nothing more than a box of relics in her dusty attic, but they had. She hated to think of Anna that way but she didn't hold out much hope these days.

Sarah often wondered, in her silent detachment from the world, if Anna was suffering at all. No longer finding any comfort from those around her, Sarah wondered if Anna was aware of how isolated she had become. She had regular visitors, true, but that was nothing compared to the fullness of the life she should have been leading. Sometimes she wondered if Anna would be better off passing quietly in her sleep so that she would never again have to remember what she had seen. There were moments when she thought, how easy it would be to reach out and take some pills from the nurse's cart that she habitually left unattended at Anna's bedside. But then she realized she wouldn't know which would be the right ones to take, the ones that would put a stop to Anna's suffering.

A few months after Peder's suicide, the Canadian police reopened the investigation into Teresa's murder, but there still wasn't any tangible link to Peder Roderick. They knew he had been in the country that night but without any physical evidence or witnesses they couldn't build a case. Besides, they said, you couldn't put a dead man on trial. Though they were right, it didn't ease the sting and Sarah wished every day that there was some way to make him pay for what he had done to her sister. What a horrible way to end such an unhappy life. Teresa had drawn the short straw with Malcolm, saddled with his mental illness, having to battled his mood swings, dodge his fits of madness. Then Anna came along and she had one bright spot in her life, only to have to leave it long before her time.

She knew she shouldn't dwell but it was hard not to imagine what life would have been like if Teresa had lived. Would she have eventually divorced Malcolm and taken Anna away? Sarah liked to think she would have, and she would have gone with her, helped take care of Anna just as she had done in the end, except then Anna would still have her mother. She also wondered if Anna's illness would have been as severe if she hadn't experienced the trauma of losing her mother. Would it have manifested itself so cruelly if she had had her mother to lean on? Of course she would never have the answers to those questions but it didn't stop her wondering.

Her Sunday visits always overlapped with Dr. Westcott's. It made her happy to see that Anna had touched her so and she gave Sarah a hug goodbye each time. Harper would busy herself taking last week's flowers out of the vase on Anna's bedside table and replacing them with fresh ones, then she would sit and crack open whatever mystery she was in the middle of reading. She never talked to Anna about the hospital. Instead she told her about growing up in Wellesley, running wild in her father's townhouse. It seemed something of a habit of people coming to visit the chronic patients to revert back to tales of happier times, simpler times.

Like Sarah, Harper wondered if Anna wouldn't be better off elsewhere. She didn't necessarily support medical suicide, but watching Anna, trapped in her traumatized mind, she certainly began to understand it. She also understood why they trained doctors not to get emotionally invested in their patients, especially in an asylum. A doctor could treat but never control how the mind might function, or break down as the case may be, and to form a friendship with a patient was to ignore the fact that something like this could happen. Losing Anna was Harper's greatest failure and she had decided that medicine was not for her, handing in her resignation after only four years at Westborough.

When Harper looked back on her years at Westborough she always thought of Anna first. She was her first heartbreak, the first case she couldn't crack. And in a way Harper felt was only fitting, she would also be the last. After saying goodbye to Anna, Dr. Westcott hung up her lab coat and went home to her father's house in Wellesley where she cashed in her trust fund and planned a trip to Europe. She would never set foot in another asylum.

One Sunday evening, after both her regular visitors had departed, Dr. Carruthers went in to check on Anna Gilman, he found her lying unnaturally still in her bed with her eyes closed, as if she was sleeping peacefully for the first time in nearly a year since she had watched her mother's killer slit his own throat right before her eyes. Dick Carruthers suspected that one of the nurses had been rather lax around Anna's visitors, leaving the medication cart unattended. When Anna died Carruthers found that she had an elevated level of morphine in her system (a drug she wasn't taking but which was kept in great number on the cart), in fact enough to incapacitate a small horse. Mixed with her daily medications it had made for a lethal cocktail.

Though Dr. Carruthers had no proof, he suspected that both Sarah Tessier and Dr. Westcott had taken pity on Anna and helped her to move on from the paralyzing fear and depression that had turned her into a veritable deaf mute. Carruthers noted the overdose in Anna's record but declined to guess at how it had happened, noting instead that she was severely underweight and likely would have starved to death shortly anyway. Part of him applauded the two women for having had the strength of will to end the suffering of someone they loved. He wasn't certain if he would have been able to had he been in that same position.

Anna Gilman was buried next to her mother on a cold, sunny day in March. Harper had conveniently departed for Europe the Monday after Anna's overdose. When she returned a month later, she found a heartfelt letter from Dr. Carruthers expressing his sympathy at the loss of her patient. Harper drove out to Pine Grove and left a bunch of wildflowers on Anna's grave, next to a bouquet of yellow roses that had been left recently, presumably by Sarah though their paths never did cross again. Harper then wrote a letter to Valerie, letting her know of Anna's passing, though she didn't expect a response, and sent it in care of Northampton State Hospital where she had heard Valerie was already making waves.

Years later Harper would attend the memorial at Northampton, the one where the German woman rigged the abandoned hospital with a sound system to play Bach's *Magnificat*. She saw Valerie in the distance, arm in arm with a dark haired woman with startling blue eyes and they were joined by a man who took Valerie's other hand and stood with them as the music started. She never did let Valerie know she was there, but it was just as well. Miss Martin had made a new life for herself and now it was time for Harper to do the same. She reached up to her breastbone and touched the diamond ring that hung there on a chain, Anna's mother's ring. It had arrived in an envelope one day, without a return address, but she knew it had come from Sarah. She found the ring inside with a note that said simply, "She would have wanted you to have this". Harper wore it every day, including the day of Sarah's funeral. She took the train out to Buffalo and was glad she did as she was the only one there to say goodbye for both her and for Anna.

As she tossed a handful of dirt and listened to the hollow ring of it against Sarah's coffin, she smiled knowing that now all three women would be together and at peace. And with any luck, Peder Roderick was rotting in hell where he belonged.

ACKNOWLEDGMENTS

Many thanks to Jessica Martin at Blue Umbrella Books for giving my books a home on her shelves. To Reggie Wilson who is at the helm of multiple branches of the Springfield City Library, thank you for bringing my book and my lecture series to so many library patrons across the city. I owe a great deal as well to Anik Sales who not only designed the cover but also served as a sounding board through the entire process. And finally to my most trusted reader Nann Halliwell whose feedback has become essential to my writing.

While this book is indeed a work of fiction, Westborough State Hospital was an active psychiatric facility in Eastern Massachusetts until its closure in 2010. Designed by Elias Carter and built in 1848 on the banks of Lake Chauncy, Westborough was one of the first asylums to institute homeopathic, or natural treatment for the mentally ill. Famed psychiatrist Solomon Carter Fuller spent the majority of his career practicing at the hospital. While there, he performed his ground-breaking research on the physical changes to the brains of Alzheimer's patients.

The former Westborough State Hospital campus currently houses active programs under the supervision of the Department of Youth Services, one of which is housed in Paine Hall.

If you haven't already, I encourage you to read *Hospital Hill* where Valerie Martin makes her first appearance. For more of my work, including my photography, visit me at www.thekatherineanderson.com.

Follow me on social media.

facebook.com/thekatherineanderson
@PoisonedPenner
@katebroderick

Made in the USA
Middletown, DE
30 July 2019